MATED TO THE *Minotaur*

a Fate's Falls cozy monster romance

KARLA DOYLE

Contents

MATED TO THE MINOTAUR

A Fate's Falls Monster Romance

When my cousin calls, distraught because her parents won't accept her fiancé because "his skin is a different color," I give her the "we ride at dawn" support she needs and deserves. Then say yes to being her maid of honor at the wedding that's in three weeks.

Booking a flight across the country and getting a dress that's "any color other than green" are doable. Making arrangements in a town Google can't locate is more challenging. Time isn't on my side and my cousin seems to be too busy to respond to messages, so I make use of the best man's contact info.

Constantine is happy to help. And his voice...it's enough to make me swoon. After one phone call, I might be more excited to meet him than I am for my cousin's wedding. I don't know what Constantine looks like, nor do I care. I'm not superficial or a racist like my cousin's parents. I'm as open-minded as it gets.

Turns out, I need to be. Fate's Falls isn't any small, mountain town—it's populated with literal monsters, including the man I'm crushing on. The hulking Minotaur could crush me in one of his massive hands. Logically, I should be scared, but I'm the opposite. I assume it's because I'm long overdue for some adventure, and more than a little curious to know if the hunky Minotaur is monstrous *all over*.

Constantine insists our connection is deeper than physical attraction. He believes we're mates. As in, fated mates. Forever.

My previously boring life just got a whole lot more interesting...

Chapter One

NATALIE

The calendar is not my friend. I have a commission piece to finish this week and I'm still in the initial sketch stage... and it's Thursday. I'll finish it before the next job is scheduled to come in, but it'd be easier if my creative mojo wasn't on an unauthorized sabbatical. I'm still getting the work done, but lately, that's how it feels —like work. I miss the days of feeling endlessly inspired. When drawing was as natural as breathing.

When did the joy of creating disappear? It's not because I'm doing commissions; I actually love drawing from a prompt. If I had to analyze it—and that's really no hardship, I'm a big fan of *over*analyzing things—I'd say my mojo left town when my parents did. We still talk almost every day, but phone calls and FaceTime aren't the same as spending time together. I miss the warm fuzzies I always get when I'm with them. That's right, I'm a twenty-eight-year-old mama's and daddy's girl. And not ashamed of that fact one little bit.

Even after they grabbed early retirement by the horns and drove off into the horizon to embrace full-time RV life, I still had Ro in my daily life. Until she, too, got hit by the wanderlust bug. Or in her case, the *lust* bug. She went on a road trip to British Columbia to meet some builder she started talking to via her online metalwork store—then stayed out there permanently. That was a year ago.

Surrounded by millions of people, yet I feel alone.

So, when the phone lights up and starts playing my cousin's ringtone, my looming deadline can suck it. Rosetta hasn't voice-called me for over two weeks. We're still best friends, but since moving to British Columbia, she's been hit-and-miss with communication. When we do talk, the reason for all the "misses" becomes apparent. She's in love. Wildly in love.

Born two days apart, we grew up together, more like sisters than cousins. Basically, we've been best friends since birth. Despite being extremely close, we're very different people. I'm the romantic, the believer in fate and fairytale endings. Ro is the "I make my own fate," try everything once, balls-out adventurous type. Minus the balls, of course. She's the va-va-voom redhead chick who turns heads no matter where she goes. And leaves a trail of broken hearts behind her.

Driving to the other side of the country to hook up with a guy she met online totally fit with her carefree nature. Putting down roots with him shocked the hell out of me. A year later, I'm still surprised every time she says she loves him. Honestly, I didn't think it'd last, no matter how great the sex is. And apparently, it's pretty great. Another way my cousin and I are opposites—she's having all the amazing sex and I'm having none. Not even bad sex.

I wait one more ring before answering. I always let it go a few before picking up. My cousin has been known to accidentally hit the *Call* button, and some of the heavy breathing I've heard because I answered scarred me for life —and made me green with envy. Unless fate sends someone directly to me, the odds of me getting *any* action are low. Like, single-digit percentage. Sadly, my life has not found its fairytale groove, and none of the men in line during my daily coffee runs have provided the epic meet-cute I know I'm destined to have. One day. One day.

"Hey, stranger," I say by way of answering. "How's the wild life?"

"Amazing. Mostly. Everything except for my idiot parents." A big, hiccupping sob comes through the line. Super out of character for Rosetta. She's cried around me exactly twice in her life—at age ten, when our grandmother on our mothers' side died, and when our grandfather followed a few months afterward.

Her parents can't be dead. If something horrible had happened to them, my mom would've called me right away. Plus, Ro would've led with that news if her parents had passed away. She wouldn't have used the word *amazing* in any sense, even though they're not close and have always butted heads.

I've often wondered if we were accidentally switched as newborns. As infants, we both had fair peach fuzz for hair and could've been twins. Hospital mix-ups happen. I'm more reserved, like her parents, whereas, she's more free-spirited, like mine. Mix-up or not, I'm glad I got my set of parents. I wouldn't trade them for anything.

"What's happening with your parents?" I ask.

"They're close-minded assholes."

That's a known fact. This isn't the first time they've clashed, and I doubt it'll be the last. "What are they being close-minded about?"

"My fiancé."

"Your *fiancé?*"

A squeal from her end of the call nearly pierces my eardrum. "Shocking, right?"

"Um, yeah! This guy must be one of a kind, getting you to put on the ball and chain. Never thought I'd see the day you'd want to commit to one person for the rest of your life. Unless—are you guys doing the open-marriage thing?"

"Hell no," she says on a riotous laugh. "Dak is not a sharer. I'm his, full stop. Even his best friend doesn't talk to me alone without letting Dak know first."

"And you're really okay with that? Being with someone so possessive? Because that's kind of got 'red flag' written all over it."

"He's possessive, not controlling. Zero red flags, I promise. Dak would do anything for me, just like I'd do anything for him. We're unbreakable."

"Ro the ho becomes the ultimate monogamist," I tease. "You sound pretty sure about it."

"I used to make fun of you for believing in finding your one true love, I know. But that saying 'when you know, you know' isn't a load of horseshit lonely people cling to. It's legit. When *the one* comes into your life, you just know."

Envy tightens its greasy fingers around my heart. "I'm happy for you, Ro, even if I haven't seen you in a year because this guy stole you from me."

Another laugh rolls into my ear. "He didn't steal me from you. You're still my favorite human in the whole world."

"Second favorite, you mean. Since your fiancé is obviously at the top of the list." The awkward silence I receive is out of character for her. I wouldn't have thought my comment problematic, but obviously, I touched a nerve. "Look, I don't care where I fall on the favorites list. If you're happy, I'm happy. I miss you so much, though! When's the big day? The wedding will be back here, I assume?" More silence. Enough to make me wonder if she's still on the call. "Ro?"

"Sorry, just calming my shit down over here because we've circled back to the asshole-parents part."

"What's their issue? They should be jumping for joy. Their 'I'm never settling down' daughter is going full-on domestic."

"Oh, they were happy I'm getting married. They didn't even care that the wedding's in three weeks, and that we're having it here."

"Wait, what?"

Ignoring me, Ro continues. "So, they asked for a video call with us, since they haven't met Dak."

That'd never happen with my parents, but they're nothing like Ro's. They're not the type to fly across the country to see their daughter and her boyfriend. Plus, they've probably been waiting for the breakup to happen—because Ro isn't the settling-down type. Or, she wasn't.

"And they didn't like him? From one video call, they made up their minds?" It wouldn't surprise me, honestly.

"They didn't even try getting to know him, Nat. The moment they saw him, they freaked out because he's not a basic white dude. They refuse to come to the wedding and say they'll disown me if I marry him."

"They're *racists?*" I whisper the despicable word even though there's nobody who could possibly hear it.

"What else do you call people who judge others by their outward appearance?"

"I'd call them a lot of things, none of them favorable." I knew my aunt and uncle were old-fashioned about a lot of things, but racist? "Do you want me to go over and try to talk sense into them?"

"No—definitely not. But there *is* something I really, *really* want you to do, if you're willing."

"Of course, Ro. Anything. Name it."

"Be my maid of honor?"

"Well, duh! Of course, I'll be your maid of honor. I'd be pissed if you chose anyone but me!"

"Ooh, Natalie gets spicy!" Ro says on a big laugh. "It suits you, babe! Keep it coming. And on the subject of coming, can you head out here early? I'll send you money for the flight. You can even upgrade to first class on my dime."

Before I can answer, she starts in on me, the way she did when we were kids. Like the times I wanted to dress up our Barbies so they could go on fancy dates with our Ken dolls in the house, but she wanted to ditch the Kens and the clothes, take naked Barbies out in the backyard, and make them do *things* with my brother's assortment of dragons and other creature figures.

"Please, please, *pleeeeease*... It'll be fun, I promise."

I couldn't say no to her then. Because I love her. Also, because I was secretly intrigued by Barbie doing unspeakable things with monsters. As for now... I can't let her down. Especially not when her parents have bailed so completely. "The fun will be in limited amounts because I have deadlines. I'll have to bring work with me. And how early is early?"

"I'll take whatever you can give me," she says. "At least a week before the wedding, though. Two would be even better."

"You said the wedding is in three weeks. So, I should drop everything and come now, basically?"

"Perfect!"

"I was kidding, Ro. Has the mountain altitude clouded your sarcasm detector?"

Her genuine laughter bubbles through the speaker. "Love has! But the air here is amazing, Nat. You'll never want to leave, trust me."

I always have, and she's never been wrong. Even about Barbie's unspeakable adventures. "Send me the info. I'll be there as soon as I can swing it."

NATALIE

There is no "instant" messaging with my cousin. She's notorious for leaving me on read, sometimes until the next day, sometimes indefinitely, because she gets distracted and forgets to reply. There's a three-hour time difference between Ontario and British Columbia, but Rosetta only gets to use that excuse when I send early-morning texts. Which I should stop doing because it only increases my frustration level. But will I change my ways? Probably not. Unlike Ro, I'm a morning person. Always have been.

Hence, why I'm up, dressed, and have put in the equivalent of half a day's work by the time the sun is rising on the west coast. I have a long to-do list before I catch my flight to Kelowna two days from now. Questions that need answering. Since my cousin isn't likely to reply in a timely fashion, I'm going with option number two—the groom's best friend and best man, Constantine. Reaching out to a total stranger for help isn't in my comfort zone, but I'd rather suffer a moment of awkwardness than the anxiety of not having plans firmly in place. Time to find out if the guy who'll be accompanying me down the aisle is an early riser.

> Hi there! 🙂 This is Natalie Somers. I'm Rosetta's cousin and her maid of honor. She gave me your number. I hope she's mentioned me and told you I might be in touch about the wedding, but with Ro, it's possible she forgot, so this might be coming out of left field… 👀 I'm hoping you can help with some long-distance planning I need to do before I head out west in a few days. You can text me or call me at this number. Thank you!

The phone rings before I can second-guess myself. I don't usually answer *Unknown* calls, but the timing would have to be a huge coincidence, so I take the chance and pick up. "Hello?"

"Hello, this is Constantine Tavros. Am I speaking with Natalie?" His voice is *so* deep. Smooth and rich, I can almost feel it wrapping around me, like midnight-blue velvet.

That's right, midnight blue. Not just any color of velvet. My brain is oddly specific about stuff like this. Also, I'm going to need Rosetta to send me a picture of this guy. For now, I'll use my imagination. He's tall, dark, handsome, and built. *All over*, of course.

"Yes, that's me," I say, pulling myself together before I end up sounding like a phone-sex operator. Notebook and pen in hand, I move from my desk chair to the couch. "Thanks for getting back to me so quickly. I know it's early there; you must be a morning person, like me. If I sound tinny, it's because I put you on speaker so I can write things down."

"Your lovely voice is perfectly clear."

Lovely? I assume he's just one of those innocently flirtatious guys, but in *his* voice, the compliment gives me the warm fuzzies *and* the tingles. It has been a while since I had a date. Even longer since I had a memorable one.

"To answer your text," he says, "I was expecting to hear from you. I told Rosetta to give you my number."

"Oh, I didn't realize. That's so thoughtful. Thank you."

A rumble even deeper than his voice comes through my phone's speaker, making it vibrate where it's propped against a cushion. It isn't a laughing rumble, nor is it an angry sound. It's something else. Something...primal.

No, Natalie, it's not. Get your head out of the bedroom, you sex-starved fool.

I give my head a shake and clear my throat as covertly as possible. "I'm sure you have things to do, so I'll try not to take much of your time."

"You're welcome to as much of my time as you want, Natalie."

Another ripple of *yes please* runs through me. Most people shorten my name to Nat, which is fine, but I like the way my full name sounds in Constantine's voice. He says it as if he's tasting it. And liking it.

"Rosetta didn't give me the name of any hotels. No matter how many internet searches I try, I haven't found a single listing for hotels, motels, or inns in Fate's Falls. I don't want to chance it by just showing up, only to find there's no vacancy anywhere. Since she didn't invite me to stay with her and Dak, I assume she had somewhere in mind, but I'm open to your suggestions."

Silence follows. Only the faint sound of breathing and a

sense of awareness I might be imagining tells me he's still on the other end of the call.

"There are no hotels, motels, or inns here," he says, finally.

"A bed-and-breakfast? A hostel with shower facilities?"

"None of those, either. Fate's Falls is a small town and fairly secluded. There's never been a need for any short-term rental places."

"Okay... can you tell me the name of the nearest town?"

More silence. Weird silence. "There are no towns nearby. We're quite isolated."

There's no logical reason for the shiver that ripples through me. So, the town's isolated. Way up in the mountains. With no accommodations for visitors. Ro lives there, and is blissfully happy, so it must be a nice place. I'm looking for trouble where none exists.

I gather a calming breath, releasing it quietly, so the man on the other end of the call won't hear it. No need for him to know I'm a chronic overthinker who's having a little internal freakout right now. "Okay, do you know where Ro planned for me to stay during the two-plus weeks I'll be there?"

"With me."

"I'm sorry, what?" There's no way I heard him correctly. Or that Rosetta would think this is okay.

"I have several empty bedrooms. I offered them to Rosetta for her family's use. As her parents have declined to attend the wedding, you'll have the largest guest bedroom and a bathroom to yourself."

"Will anyone else be there? Your wife? Girlfriend?

Boyfriend? Parents? Kids? Other boarders?" I clamp my mouth shut before any more rambling escapes.

"I have no romantic attachments, no children, and my parents live out of town. I live alone, and there will be no other guests. Only the two of us. But I have a large home. You'll have as much privacy as you want."

Just me and the deep-voiced stranger—who happens to be single and nobody's baby daddy—alone in his house for two weeks. I should politely decline, say goodbye, then call Ro and put her on blast. Either she lets me sleep on her couch, or I bow out of the wedding. Not an unreasonable request, unlike what she expects from me. This *huge* thing she didn't even tell me about, choosing to let Constantine drop the bomb instead. She's in so much shit when I see her. So. Much. Shit.

"It's incredibly generous and kind of you, opening your home up, especially for a lengthy stay. Let me know how much I can give you for your hospitality."

"I don't want your money, Natalie." Somehow, his voice sounds even deeper. The comment is innocent, but the way he says it...

I would swear there's silent innuendo in those words. Like, he doesn't want my money, but he wants something else. Something my body is all tingly about. Which is ridiculous because I have never met this man. I know nothing about him, have no idea what he looks like. His voice, though—I know I like that.

"Have you reserved a rental car at the airport?" he asks.

"Yes, one with all-wheel drive, even though it's summer. Rosetta said there's a lot of uphill driving, and some roads are on the rough side. She hasn't given me directions, but I'm sure the rental will have GPS."

"Some of these small mountain towns don't show up in the satellite mapping. I'll send you detailed directions that'll bring you to the main road into town. There's an outpost there, and it's a good spot for us to meet. After that, you can follow me into town. And if you run into any confusion along the way, I'm just a phone call away."

"Wow, you really take this 'best man' job seriously."

His chuckle is warm and genuine, and I find myself biting my lip to hide a smile he can't see. "Helping people is always a pleasure for me, never a job."

"You must be single by choice." The comment is hanging in the air as fast as it entered my mind. "Sorry, *that* thought was supposed to stay *inside* my head. It's none of my business why you're not romantically attached."

Another deep and delicious chuckle comes through my phone's little speaker. "I'll tell you anything you want to know. Ask away."

"Tempting," I say, switching to handset mode so I can have his voice directly in my ear. "But I should probably save the personal questions until we've known each other longer than a few minutes via a long-distance phone call."

"I'm looking forward to that."

"Me too." Because he seems nice. That's all. Not because I've developed a sight-unseen insta-crush on some guy I know next to nothing about. "Oh, I think you have another call waiting," I say, when a muted double-beep sounds in the air between us. "I'll let you go so you can take it."

"It can go to voicemail—unless you need to get going."

"I don't. I'm a freelancer and work from home. Nobody's clocking my break time."

"Rosetta has shown me some of your work online. Impressive. You're a talented artist."

"Thank you."

Interesting. There are only two reasons Ro would talk about me to her fiancé's friend. One, because she needed to, since the man is offering to house me in his guest room. Or two, because she's got matchmaking in mind. I should hope it's the first option. *Should.*

"I wish I could say I know something about you," I say, "but when Ro and I talk, it's usually about her and Dak. Honestly, looking him in the eye, knowing the things I know, is going to be a struggle."

Constantine's rumbling laugh sends ripples of heat through me. "Do me a favor and don't share any of that information with me."

"So, you don't want to know about the dildo set Dak sent for her to—"

"Stop," he says through a choking laugh. "Show some mercy for the guy who *does* have to look Dak in the eye later."

Light laughter bubbles up from my chest as naturally as breathing. This is nice. I can't remember the last time I found it this easy to talk to someone new. And to a man who interests me—never. Probably because this is a zero-pressure situation. Even if I find Constantine attractive when I meet him, even if he feels the same and we have amazing chemistry, it wouldn't lead anywhere. We live thousands of kilometers apart. But a short-term fling while I'm out there... that's a possibility. If I can pause overthinking long enough to let it happen. Going to have to fight my nature for that to happen.

And now I've gotten *way* ahead of myself. "Do you work with Dak in his construction business?" I ask, wiggling down into my collection of throw pillows, some of which are midnight-blue velvet. Not that that's a sign or anything.

"I help with heavy lifting when he needs an extra pair of hands, but that's the extent of my involvement. My line of work is less grueling. I own a couple of businesses in town. *The Brew* is a coffeehouse in the daytime and a brewpub in the evening. My other business is related—it's a small-batch craft brewery called *Bullheaded Brew*."

"Wow, that's amazing. Were they turnkey businesses, or did you start them from scratch?"

"Scratch, but with a lot of community support. We're big on that in Fate's Falls."

"Rosetta always says it's incredible there. It's the one thing she finds time to slide into her otherwise X-rated conversations."

"Which you're not going to tell me about."

"No." I giggle. "Not until my last day there, anyway."

"Maybe you'll fall in love with the place like your cousin did, and you won't have a last day here."

"Ro fell in love with a person, not a place. She would've been happy to live anywhere with Dak." Hopefully, the envy in my voice isn't as obvious to Constantine as it is to my ears.

"He's completely dedicated to her also, if you had any doubts."

"I don't know him at all yet, but I don't have doubts.

Ro has gushed about Dak since they were still in the long-distance talking stage. I'm shocked she's settling down with one person for the rest of her life, but she's madly in love with him, so I'm happy for her."

"What about you?" he asks. "Your cousin says you aren't involved with anyone. Are you in the 'single by choice' category like Rosetta used to be, with no desire to settle down?"

Again, why is Ro talking about me to her fiancé's buddy? It's one thing to tell him how I spend my workdays. Totally another to tell him how I'm *not* spending my free time.

"No, Ro and I were never in the same dating category. Even when we were little, we wanted different things. While her Barbie dolls were out doing the wild thing with wild things, mine always put on the white gown and walked down the aisle. And now she's walking down the aisle."

"And you're out doing the wild thing?"

The snort that bursts from me couldn't be less delicate if I tried. And I did it directly into the phone's microphone. Because, of course, I couldn't have done that while I had him on speaker.

"I take it that's a no," he says, chuckling. At least he didn't seem to mind my unfeminine noise.

Not that I should care, one way or another, but I'm relieved he didn't recoil. "No, I'm a diehard 'white picket fence' girl. I may never find Mr. Right, but I'd rather be alone than work my way through a string of Mr. Wrongs." A brief, awkward laugh involuntarily leaves me. "Not very optimistic or exciting, I know."

"Nothing wrong with choosing to wait for the right person."

"Oh—no, I'm not *waiting*, waiting. Not the big waiting. You know what I mean, right?" God, I hope so. I really don't want the deep-voiced man I'm going to be bunking with to think I'm a twenty-eight-year-old virgin, saving herself for *the one*. That'd really put a damper on any potential fling.

"I know what you mean, yes." No outright chuckle this time, but his tone definitely leans toward amusement.

"I should probably exit this conversation before I divulge any other embarrassing details of my life. But I'm looking forward to meeting you, and seeing everything Fate's Falls has to offer in the weeks I'm there. On that subject, is there a salon in town where I can make a hair and nail appointment for the wedding? I asked Ro, but like the hotel thing, she failed to answer. I know she's excited and busy and stressed, but all I'm going to be is stressed if I don't get some firm plans in place."

"I'll send the salon's number over with the driving directions. Need anything else? Dress shop? Shoe store?"

"I have my dress and shoes already, but do you know if any of the local shops sell lingerie?" I should tell him I'm asking because I haven't had a chance to buy my cousin a bridal shower gift, but when his deep rumble fills my ear again, I bite my tongue. I really like that sound.

Another call-waiting beep makes itself known on his end, and this time, he doesn't brush it off. "That's my manager at the coffeehouse calling from her personal number. She wouldn't call unless it's important, so I better take it."

"Of course. Thank you for all your help."

"We'll talk again soon, Natalie." The confidence in his smooth voice sends another little thrill through me.

Fortunately, he ends the call before my breathy "bye" slips out. I'm not a superficial person, but I should at least see a picture of the man before I work myself up too much. Except, I don't want Ro to send me a picture of Constantine. Pictures aren't always an accurate representation of who someone is. When I see him for the first time, I want it to be real. Personal.

When I woke up this morning, I was panicking about *only* having two days before flying out to British Columbia. Now, those two days are going to seem like the longest ever.

Chapter Two

CONSTANTINE

The addition Dakgorim is building is sided with wide wood planks milled from local trees. Today, he's installing windows and French doors that open toward what was once wild forest, but is now a manicured clearing, complete with a fenced-in area where his future children will play. The addition to his home, the one he now shares with Rosetta, is a nursery.

I'm happy for him, but envious. As full as my life is, it still has a void. One that can only be filled by a mate.

"Looking good," I call, from across the yard.

Neither the compliment nor the notice of my approach are necessary. Dak knows his craftsmanship is top-notch, and the big orc's hearing is even better than mine. Like Minotaurs and many other non-human creatures, orcs have heightened senses. We also share the need to live in secrecy.

Humans have lower levels of vision, hearing, strength, and various other qualities than most "monsters," yet they are our greatest threat.

Not all humans, of course. A number of them live among us in Fate's Falls, including Dak's mate, his soon-to-be bride. Gauging humans' intentions based on appearance was possible many centuries ago. Not now. They no longer favor pitchforks and torches for their attacks. If it were only fear because we're different, it could be managed. The real danger lies in humans' desire to capitalize on our species' differences, and technology has given them the means to be stealthy and targeted in their aggression.

To exist in peace requires hiding in places humans can't access—something nearly impossible in this day and age. Towns like Fate's Falls, shielded and governed by very old, powerful magic, allow us to hide in plain sight.

Grateful as I am for our safe haven, living within the protected boundaries makes it difficult to connect with new people. Not an issue for those who desire solitude or have already found their mate, neither of which applies to me. Platonic and casual relationships were enough until I reached prime breeding age. Now, the urge to be with my one true mate has made living without her very...uncomfortable.

Dakgorim doesn't pause when I reach him. He doesn't even look up, just continues working. Head down, focused, unstoppable. He's been that way all the years I've known him. But this project has him wound tighter than I've ever seen.

"At this rate, you'll be done before the wedding," I say

as he lifts a large window into the framed opening with ease.

He grunts, narrowing his eyes at me. "I will finish before Rosetta's cousin arrives."

There's only one reason that would be necessary. "Do you need the room finished because Natalie's staying here?"

Dak's lips curl in a way only an orc's can. A terrifying expression, but I know it's involuntary, not intentional. "This room is for our child, not...*guests*." He says the last word as if it's unpleasant. To him, it probably is. Before Rosetta entered his life, Dak kept to himself. If I hadn't essentially bullied him into friendship years ago, it wouldn't have happened. "Rosetta wishes to use the nursery to tell her cousin about our unborn orcling. She would have been happy with the framed structure, but I will ensure it is completed."

No surprise there. Dak has worshipped the ground Rosetta walks on since she set foot in Fate's Falls. True to his orc nature, he's also very possessive of the ground under Rosetta's feet, the air she breathes, etcetera. Hence why I'm out here talking to him when he's not the person I need to speak with.

Since I *am* out here with him, I can't help replaying parts of my conversation with Natalie earlier. I cut Natalie off from going into detail, but I have a pretty good idea why Dak would've sent Rosetta a set of dildos. Orcs are much larger than humans. In every way, including the size of their cocks.

The same can be said of Minotaurs. As much as my hope for a relationship with Natalie makes me curious about how Dak and his fiancée handle their disproportionate anatomies, I can't broach the subject. Natalie and I will have to find our own way in the bedroom—if we get there at all. Even though I know she's my mate, it's still possible she'll take one look at me and run as far away as possible.

"Did you come all the way out here to stare into the forest?" Dak's voice snaps me from my thoughts. He hasn't stopped working to speak to me, but his attention darts between the level he's checking and my face. "Perhaps you should sell that too-large house in town and have me build you a one-bedroom cottage with a nice view of the pine trees." It could be a legitimate offer, or Dak's particular brand of dry sarcasm. Likely a bit of both.

"I came out here to talk to Rosetta about her cousin."

Thick eyebrows rise over eyes so dark they're impossible to read. "She is in her workshop. I do not allow her in the construction area. Her safety is paramount, especially now."

We both know his use of *do not allow* isn't literal. Rosetta may be petite, but her attitude is far from small. If she wanted to hang around and watch him build the nursery, she would. Of course, then he'd stop working on the addition to build some sort of safety station to protect her from all the things he deems hazardous. That's probably why she abides his request to stay out. Well, that and the near-seamless way their dynamic fits together.

I've only taken a single step toward the large, rectangular outbuilding that houses Rosetta's metal-working shop and Dak's construction equipment when he says, "Your respect is appreciated."

Pivoting, I give him a nod. Even an orc's best man

knows better than to approach his mate without permission. Formality out of the way, I continue on to the shop.

Because of the noisy machinery, a loud chime sounds and lights flash when I open the door. Safety precautions Dak installed when Rosetta began doing her metalworking in here.

Rosetta kills the power at her workstation, sets her cutting tool down, and flips her safety visor up. "Hey, Constantine. What's up?"

"Your cousin contacted me this morning. By text. I responded by calling."

"Not surprised." She glances at my hands. "I don't know how guys like you and Dak use cellphones at all, since they're all made for human hands. One of your fingers takes up half the screen's width."

"I use a stylus for texting. But I called Natalie because I wanted to talk with her as directly as possible, so she'd feel more comfortable staying in my home." I would never use an ill-tempered tone with Dak's mate, but I do cross my arms across my chest. "A plan she wasn't aware of."

"Oh, yeah, about that..." She shrugs and raises her hands, palms up. "Oopsie?"

"Unconvincing."

"You're right. I totally avoided answering questions that might cause her to cancel her trip. She's been my best friend since we were born, and she's the only member of my family who'll be at my wedding. I couldn't risk it."

"You weren't concerned that having a man she's never met tell her she'll be living with him for two weeks might bring her plans to a screeching halt?"

"Any other man, yes. But I knew you'd have no problem wooing her."

"Convincing her, you mean."

"No, I meant *wooing* her." Rosetta moves away from the vise holding a strip of metal with three pieces of rebar protruding upward. She leans one hip against the end of the workbench and mimics my folded-arms stance. "I saw the way you looked at her picture on her website's bio page. There are plenty of beautiful females in Fate's Falls, and I've never seen you get moon-eyed over anyone. Hell, I've been here for a year and you've never gone on a single date, that I'm aware of."

"That's correct, I have not." And it's been a lot longer than a year.

"I knew it." She nods at the verification. "Tell me you didn't go home and immediately stalk Nat's socials."

"I didn't." I huff out a breath when she narrows her gaze. "Not immediately. I had to stop at the brewery and do some work first."

"Ha! I knew it."

"Natalie is very attractive."

The snorted laugh Rosetta makes is similar to Natalie's during our telephone conversation this morning. I found Natalie's adorable. Charming. Rosetta's has no effect on me whatsoever.

"Do you disagree?" I ask.

"Oh, no. She's beautiful. It's the way you said her name that made me chuckle. *Nat-a-lie...* each syllable drawn out, like it's the prettiest name you've ever had the privilege to say. All reverent and shit."

"It is a lovely name."

Rosetta removes the welding helmet and sets it aside. Her red hair sticks out in every direction, having long since escaped a bun, and she makes no attempt to smooth it. "Look, there's no denying you're the reigning Mr. Congeniality in Fate's Falls, but let's be real here, okay? Just between us girls," she winks, "you've got a little crush on my cousin, don't you?"

"I do not have a crush. I'm intrigued. At this point in my life, I should only be attracted to one woman."

"And you're attracted to a bunch? Look, I've been there. I used to have my eyes on lots of guys at the same time, so I'm not judging. But that won't sit well with Nat. Even short-term. She's not boring or a prude, but she is traditional. Definitely someone who wants to stay inside the white picket fence, not someone who plays the field. You're a good friend to Dak and me, and I like you, but I don't want Nat to get hurt. So, this is me asking you to look elsewhere, instead of at my maid of honor. In fact, I'll head into town now, before the dayshift ends at *The Brew*. I know Dela has a one-bedroom apartment, but she's a sweetheart. I bet she'll let Nat crash on her couch for a couple of weeks."

"No," I say, blocking her forward motion. Totally out of character for me, and the wide-eyed expression on Rosetta's face is enough to make me step aside immediately. "I apologize. And now I'm requesting you don't find other accommodations for your cousin."

"Give me a good reason not to. How do I know I can trust you with the closest thing I have to a sister?"

"Because when I said I should only be attracted to one woman, I meant that I am only *able* to be attracted to one woman. Once a Minotaur reaches a certain point of maturity, our biology demands we find our mate. I reached that age fifteen years ago, and haven't been attracted to anyone since. Believe me, I've tried, I've looked—a decade and a half is a long time to go without...companionship. I don't get to choose my mate; Minotaur pairings are governed by innate forces. By fate. I'm attracted to Natalie—and only to Natalie."

"Are you saying what I think you're saying? You think she's your fated mate? From looking at a picture?"

There's no way I'm telling her it began earlier than that. "Any doubts I had disappeared when I heard her voice."

For a moment, Rosetta covers her mouth with her hand. Then she shakes both out at her sides. "Shit, she's going to freak the fuck out."

"Because I'm a Minotaur."

"Well, yeah, that's part of it. I haven't told her there are non-humans here, or that I'm in love with an orc. All I said is that my parents disapprove of Dak because of his skin color. Which is not a lie," she says, raising her index finger. "But I think she's going to be okay with the whole 'monsters are real' jazz once she stops hyperventilating and meets everyone."

"Then why do you believe she'll freak out about being my mate? Both you and Natalie have told me she's a permanent, committed-relationship type of person. Wouldn't that make her inclined toward a positive response?"

"She wants a happily ever after, but she's planning to *choose* who she spends her life with, not be *told* she's someone's fated mate."

"Do you feel you chose Dak? That finding each other had nothing to do with fate and your mate bond?"

Though he's not one to engage in extended or deeply personal conversation, Dakgorim has stated a firm belief that fate led him to find Rosetta's online metalworks shop. At the time, he had no projects that required unique, hand-made metal fixtures, yet he searched the internet for such, anyway. And found Rosetta's creations—and his mate.

In front of me, Rosetta makes a sound that's part sigh, part harrumph, the noise accompanied by a narrowed gaze and hands on her hips. "This has nothing to do with Dak and me."

Meaning, I've made my point. But this isn't the time to gloat or tease. I need Rosetta's support, not her ire.

"Even if Nat is attracted to you," Rosetta continues, "she's only going to be in town for a couple of weeks. Boring as I think her life in Toronto is, she's a creature of routine. I had no issue packing up and changing venues, but I don't see her uprooting from everything she's known for twenty-eight years to stay here. Plus, it sucks that my parents are dicks and I may never speak to them again, but it's not even a sacrifice to me because I have my life with Dak. Nat, on the other hand, is super tight with her parents. There's no way she'd lie to them, or give them up—either or both of which she'd have to do if she moved her to be with you. I'm sorry, Constantine, but there's no way she can be your fated mate."

Arguing is pointless. But I know the truth. There's no way Natalie Somers *isn't* my fated mate.

CONSTANTINE

The people who work in my businesses are incredibly good at their jobs, and my presence is rarely required. I hired Shay Winterlock when she moved to Fate's Falls. *The Brew* was relatively new back then, still in its first year of operation, and only a coffeehouse at that time. In the beginning, I worked in the business full-time. Didn't matter that I, the owner, was on-site and technically the manager. Shay quickly assumed the role. She saw ways to improve operations and forged forward without permission or assistance, tweaking things to make them more appealing, efficient, or profitable. She's a doer whose decisions always have a positive effect.

Fifteen years later, I still drop in at *The Brew* a couple days a week, but spend most of that time in the kitchen or back office. Shay and Dela keep the customer-facing side running like a well-oiled machine. My bulky presence behind the counter tends to be more of a hindrance than a help.

Today's visit isn't about offering to help or staying out of the way.

Mid-afternoon is a steady time. A continual but light flow of customers, nobody in a hurry, generally speaking. There are three people in line when I enter through the front door. A shapeshifter named Trace from the outpost, Razbunare, a vengeance demon who I'm sure is here to soak up Dela's presence more than he's here for the coffee, and Lexi, the little witch who owns *Every Witch Way*, an online sex-toy business that's earning a tidy residual income for many of Fate's Falls residents.

I give them all a casual wave as I pass, then head behind the counter toward Shay, where she's cleaning an espresso machine as if the equipment needs plague-level decontamination. "Did we have another malfunction since you called this morning?"

There's not much Shay can't handle without me, which is why I cut my call with Natalie short this morning, when Shay called for a second time. Our usual tech wasn't picking up when she tried him. She was this-close to asking one of the larger customers in line to carry the possessed piece of equipment out to the back alley.

"No. The new guy you got came by and fixed it. No problems since." The straight-lipped expression on Shay's face suggests there is a problem, even it it's unrelated to the earlier mechanical issue.

After a decade and a half, I'd say we're more than employer and employee. Friends on a level that includes mutual trust and concern, but not close enough to socialize or share our internal stuff. Not close enough that I feel comfortable asking what's wrong, even though it's obvious something is. Maybe she'll talk to Dela later. They seem to have become good friends since Dela moved to town seven months ago.

A glance over my shoulder confirms Dela has the customer traffic under control. Clearing my throat to prepare for the uncomfortable reason I'm here causes me to huff in a distinctly Minotaur way.

Shay's attention snaps up to my face. "You okay, boss?"

"Yes. No. I hope so."

Her green eyes open wide, all traces of irritation gone from her face. "This is a first. You're not one to hang around in the gray zone. I take it there's some way I can help, but you hate being in a position to ask for it."

"Exactly."

She waits a few beats, grinning when all I manage to get out is another bullish huff of breath. "You're going to have to tell me. I'm not a mind reader."

"But you are a seer, and that's the help I'm here to ask for."

Smile, gone. Green eyes, shuttered hard. "Then I can't help you."

"I know you don't like to use your magic—"

She cuts me off with a raised hand. "Remove the words 'like to' from that sentence. I *don't* use my magic. Period. By choice—my choice."

If anyone in town knows the reason Shay turned away from magic, I've never heard about it. "I apologize for overstepping." Seems like my day for that. Another damn huff escapes while I'm rubbing the back of my neck. Embarrassed as I am that my bullish nature is getting the best of me, the involuntary response appears to take the edge off of Shay's intensity.

"Let's finish this conversation in the office," she says, then cranes her neck to see around me, toward Dela. "I'll just be a few minutes."

"No problem," Dela says, as cheerfully as always.

Shaking my head at Shay, I wave off the opportunity of a private conversation. If I can't say it to her out here, it should probably remain unsaid, as my request should have. "No need, thank you. And I sincerely regret asking what I did. I've got something important coming up, and I'm in unfamiliar territory. Guess I just wanted a cheat code, to make sure I'm on the right path."

Shay gives a small laugh. "There are no cheat codes. Even if I used my powers, I might not get the answer to whatever your specific question is. I never know what part of someone's future I'll see when I touch them. But if you want to *talk*, run your concerns past me, I'll give you my unbiased opinion. That's a skill I'm always willing to share."

My turn to laugh now. Interesting as Shay's unbiased opinion about my situation might be, I'm not going there. "Appreciate it, thanks. But it's probably best I let things unfold however fate intends."

"Wise choice. No point fighting fate."

With every cell of my being telling me my mate will soon be part of my life, I couldn't agree more. All I can do now is wait and hope Natalie feels the same way.

Two days later

CONSTANTINE

Since our first conversation two days ago, I've spent more time on the phone with Natalie than I have with everyone I know combined, probably for the past year, if not longer.

She replied to my emailed driving directions by saying how much she enjoyed talking to me, and suggested I call her again, anytime. Fortunately, I was alone when I read that message, because I celebrated the invitation with a bellowing rumble. Then wasted no time accepting the invitation. I called her later that day and we talked for an hour. About her art. My businesses. Conversation came easily and the minutes flew by. I only let her go when she sighed and said she had to buckle down and finish a commission piece so she could stay on schedule, adding that she was already stressed-out because she was running late.

If she were here, with our mate bond established, I would do everything within my power to ensure she never experienced stress. She wouldn't have to take on more work than she can comfortably accomplish. She wouldn't have to *work* at all. I would happily provide for all her needs, so she had time to create whatever she wanted, on her own timeline. And I would satisfy all of her intimate needs. Even without meeting her in person, I know we'll have chemistry in the bedroom. Fate wouldn't pair us if we weren't compatible in every possible way.

After saying goodbye at the end of our second conversation, I resisted the urge to call her again later that night. With her impending work deadline, the three-hour time difference, and knowing she's an early riser, I was surprised when her name lit my phone as I was settling in bed for the night. Talking to her while I lay naked in the dark made it impossible to keep my hand off my cock, which hardened the moment I heard her voice. I ended up taking our conversation to the living room, with all the lights on, to keep the growling need out of my voice. Even after an hour of conversation about our favorite foods, recreational activities, and other innocent topics, I was still hard for her.

The following day brought a couple more phone calls. The first one, brief and casual. The nighttime one leaned into flirtatious territory—on both our parts. Subtle comments. Suggestive meanings. Though it wasn't a long conversation, it ended with a deep rumble I couldn't contain and I'm sure she heard. And from her end, a breathy goodnight that left me no choice but to take the edge off after the call. I've never come so fast in my life.

This morning, I awoke to a text she'd sent in the wee hours, after checking in for her red-eye to Kelowna.

She was in the air with her phone powered off by the time I saw the message. I replied immediately, telling her it's not awkward and I feel the same way about her. Then I sent a separate text to let her know Rosetta and I would meet her at the outpost I'd noted in my directions.

Rosetta wasn't part of my original plan. Having her there is insurance. A way to soften the shock that might cause Natalie to get into her rental car and drive straight back to the airport after seeing me. Because I don't know what I'd do if that happened.

Natalie texted when she landed; just a quick one to let me know she was safely on the ground and headed my way. No more mention of her excitement to see me, but the triple blushing face emojis were a good sign. Women have a definite advantage when it comes to emojis.

"You're awfully quiet over there," Rosetta says from the passenger seat of my pickup truck, where we're parked at the outpost.

The outpost sits just outside of Fate's Falls and is staffed by shapeshifters. They predominantly assume human form while manning the station. Most of the time, their job consists of coordinating deliveries with our in-town drivers, since all mail and packages are processed through the outpost. Sometimes the outpost staff act in a park ranger capacity, redirecting travelers who've taken a wrong turn on the mountain roads. They never have to act in a security capacity because only those approved by the Oracle are able to pass the boundary. Those who aren't won't even see the road leading into town.

"You're quiet too," I say, keeping my eyes on the empty road ahead.

"I guess we're both nervous about Nat's reaction. Maybe I should've met her here by myself, instead of with you."

That would've required Rosetta making the offer, which she didn't, but now isn't the time to point out her lack of consideration where Natalie's travel plans are concerned.

"I'm surprised you didn't pick Natalie up at the airport," I say instead, though it's another criticism that's been on my mind since Rosetta told me her cousin was coming to Fate's Falls for the wedding, and that she hadn't disclosed we're a town full of non-humans.

"Because I want the baby news to happen at my house, and I knew I wouldn't be able to hold it in during the long drive, during which Nat would undoubtedly ask a million questions."

"Understandable. I've talked to her a lot in the past couple of days, but always making sure I steer the conversation away from anything that could lead to questions I don't want to answer honestly until we're face-to-face."

Rosetta gives a small, commiserative smile. "Soon it'll all be out in the open."

"And you firmly believe Natalie will accept everything she's about to discover?"

"If I didn't, I wouldn't have asked her to take a five-hour flight across the country, followed by an hours-long drive into the mountains to a town she wouldn't have been able to see or enter." Rosetta's mouth twitches from side to side, then she sighs. "Okay, I haven't fully disclosed everything to *you* either. I consulted the Oracle before I called Nat. I had to know if she'd be allowed past the boundary to attend my wedding."

"That was very responsible of you."

She rolls her eyes. "I'm not *completely* self-absorbed."

"Of course not," I say, though it's not a completely honest opinion. Rosetta merrily goes about her life without pausing to consider others, the exception being Dak. She has always prioritized his happiness. That gets her a pass in my books. "With the wedding and baby stuff, taking that preemptive measure with the Oracle could easily have fallen through the cracks."

She narrows her gaze at me. *"Riiight."* Self-absorbed though she may be, she's still damn perceptive when she pays attention. She knows I'm being consciously neutral. Sucking up, if you will.

"What did the Oracle say?" I withhold the other question I want to ask—why she didn't tell me this information sooner. As in, during our conversation in her workshop two days ago, when I revealed that Natalie is my mate.

"The Oracle said there are no visitor passes for Fate's Falls. For a being as old as time itself, she's pretty snappy. Doesn't miss a beat."

"What else did the Oracle say?"

"What makes you think there was more?" Rosetta's intentional torment and obvious amusement in dishing it causes my tail to whip upward. She glances at it in the space between us in the front seat. "I always forget you have a tail, but not during this little blip of a trip."

Tail movement is primarily involuntary, and more noticeable when emotions are heightened. Everything has been running higher since I spoke with Natalie. All of my instinctual Minotaur traits are amplified.

When my only response is a bullish huff, Rosetta laughs, at which my tail whips sharply to the right.

"It's pretty. So floofy at the end."

"It is not *pretty*. Or... *floofy*."

"Chill, Constantine, your masculinity is intact; I was only talking about your tail. But you know what?" She twists on her seat, tapping her cheek while her gaze wanders over my clenched-jaw expression. "Now that I'm stuck in this truck with you, getting a good, up-close look, your hair is pretty, too. So shiny. Looks like you don't have a single split end on those long, wavy locks. Tell me your beauty secrets. Do you deep condition?"

There's no withholding yet another gruff release of breath, this one louder than the last. "Is this how you speak to Dakgorim?"

"God, no. He'd lose his shit. But I have told him he's cute plenty of times. And sexy, of course."

I can't imagine the word *cute* sits well with the massive, permanently scowling orc, and I have no desire to lead her into further conversation about his *sexiness*.

"Oh, look, there's a car coming!" Rosetta sits up

straight, pointing at the road beyond the windshield. "That has to be Nat."

The minor irritation Rosetta stirred up vanishes, replaced by a buzz of anticipation. With each second, my heart beats faster, harder. My body and soul know my mate is nearby. My wait is almost over.

Chapter Four

NATALIE

Thank goodness Constantine sent detailed directions. He told me some of the small mountain towns don't show up on the satellite map and he was right. There were no results when I typed "Fate's Falls" into my rental car's GPS. Literally none.

I love Rosetta like a sister and a best friend, but Constantine's number is the only useful information she's given me for this trip. Her text replies have fallen into three categories: brief, evasive, and emoji. Not a big deal if I were back home, going about my normal, predictable life. But I'm here, thousands of kilometers from my safe little studio apartment on the third floor. I'm driving up an actual mountain, on a narrow road bordered by trees as tall as my apartment building. Maybe taller.

If I took a wrong turn or had some sort of freak automotive failure, I'd be screwed. There hasn't been a single town since I began my ascent. But there have been plenty of wildlife warning signs. Deer. Moose. Bears. No thank you to those and all others. I'm not a fan of big furry things.

So, yes, I'm a bit peeved with my cousin for leaving me hanging. For potentially putting my life in danger. Even so, I'm still relieved she's going to be there with Constantine when I arrive.

I haven't stopped thinking about my phone calls with him. It's likely I've built our connection up in my head, made more of it than it actually is. Rationally, I blame my recent lack of dating. Of course, I'd respond to a friendly, helpful, deep-voiced man. I'm only human.

Still, we spent hours on the phone the past couple of days. He called multiple times. We texted too. They weren't just casual conversations between two people whose best friends are getting married. Honestly, we barely even talked about Ro and Dak. We talked about my art, his businesses, our likes and dislikes for lots of day-to-day stuff. Lots of getting to know each other. Yet, even from the first call, it felt as if I already know him.

The way we connected so naturally... that's how I've always expected a real relationship to feel. The long-term, there's no doubt it's going to last forever, kind.

I definitely need to leave my apartment more. Interact with people, face-to-face. Put myself out there, in the dating trenches, until I find somebody I'm comfortable with. Someone who'll be easy to talk to *and* give me tingly feelings. Somebody like Constantine.

Sighing, I glance at my phone where it's sitting in the dashboard mount I brought along. According to the route I manually programmed into the map app, the Fate's Falls' outpost should be directly ahead.

"Continue on this road for five-hundred meters, then your destination is on the right." By the time the artificial voice has finished her instructions, there's a single-story building within view.

I assumed it'd be small gatehouse at the edge of town. I assumed wrong. The closer I get, the larger I realize it is. The front portion of the building looks like a log cabin—like an old-time outpost—but the rear section is sided with metal and there are two large bay doors, the kind you'd see on a warehouse. This isn't just a security guard's station for a gated community.

Maybe I'm in the wrong place. Seems unlikely, given the specific directions I received, but out here in the middle of nowhere, it kind of feels like anything is possible.

Heart racing, I pull into the parking lot, the gravel crunching under my tires as I park across from the only other vehicle in the lot—a large, dark, four-door pickup truck. With its tinted windows and the sunlight shining in my eyes, I can't make out the passengers in the front seat of the cab. I hold my foot on the brake pedal and keep the engine running.

My pulse kicks even higher as the truck's passenger door opens. Then everything in the world is right because my cousin is running across the parking lot, waving her arms, calling my name. I put the car in *park* and turn off the engine, hopping out as she reaches the driver's door of my rental.

"You're here!" Squealing, she pulls me into a hug before I can even close the car door, bouncing me around in a semi-circle before releasing me and standing back, still holding my hands. "I didn't realize how much I missed you, but holy shit, I've missed you!"

"You've been too busy being in love to miss me, which I'm very happy about, and I'm sure your parents will be, eventually, too."

The twist of her previously smiling lips tells me I should've left her parents out of this reunion moment.

"Sorry. Forget I mentioned them. The next couple of weeks are all about you," I say, checking her over, head to toe, then back again. "Mountain air, love, and constant boinking agree with you, Ro. You're practically glowing."

A laugh lighter than the brilliant sunshine overhead floats from her fresh smile. "I have literally never been happier. And every day when I wake up, I'm even happier than the day before. I didn't know life could be like this."

I should be overjoyed for her, not overflowing with jealousy. Green is not a good color for me. I'll get over it. A deep-voiced distraction would help, though. "Is Constantine just going to wait in the truck?" I ask, attempting to twist around to face the vehicle that's now behind me. "I know you're going to think this sounds silly, but we've talked a lot the past few days, and I'm excited to meet him in person."

Rather than let me shift position, Ro blocks me. "It's not silly at all, and I know he's super excited about meeting you, too, but there's something I need to tell you before he comes over."

"What is it? God, Ro, you should see your face. It must be horrible. Is he—" *No.* I refuse to say any of the superficial words aloud. "Is his great personality compensating for something beyond his control? It has to be something external if you think you have to prepare me for it. You wouldn't have me staying at his house if he's a monster."

Ro makes a strangled sound, her fair complexion burning bright red. "Boy, do you know how to pick the words." Shaking her head, she retrieves her phone from her jeans' pocket, swipes and taps a few times, then takes a deep breath. "First, I'll show you a picture of my fiancé."

"Seriously? You're going to dangle that mysterious comment, then leave me hanging while you show me a picture of your fiancé?" This is getting weirder by the minute. I already know Dak's not a garden-variety white guy, otherwise her parents wouldn't have taken issue with his skin color.

Constantine must be the same nationality as her fiancé. Though, why she thinks she needs to ease me into it is beyond me. There's not a racist bone in my body. She knows that. Probably better than anyone.

I can't help cracking a smile when she hands me the phone, displaying what's obviously a Halloween party picture. "He's really tall and built like a brick shithouse—definitely your type. It's great that you found someone with a fun-loving personality to match yours. But why aren't you in costume, too?"

"I'm not in costume because he's not in costume." Her expression is stone-cold serious when I look up from the image. "He's an orc. For real."

"Very funny, Ro."

"Scroll backward and forward. You'll see."

There's no way she's serious. She's setting me up for something.

"Nice try. No matter how much you rave about it, I do not want to see a picture of his dick. I'm happy to accept your word for it being enormous."

"You have to see it to truly believe it, but you're just going to have to take my word for it because there are no pictures of Dak's dick." She makes a swiping motion with her finger. "Scroll."

"I just flew across the country, then drove up a damn mountain. I'm exhausted. Too drained to joke around. Can we please just go into town so I can clean up and relax? We can play your 'I'm marrying a big green monster' game later."

"Just scroll," she says, sighing. "Please."

"Fine." Since I'm already expecting more of the man-in-costume pics, it doesn't surprise me when that's what I see. Except, there are a lot. Like, *a lot*.

Based on the backgrounds and Ro's various outfits, the pictures span multiple seasons. Her clothes range from her shop coveralls to jeans and sweaters, a puffy parka, shorts and tiny tanks, and plaid pajamas. There's even one where they're both wearing dressier clothes—Ro in a body-hugging purple dress and him in black slacks and a dress shirt. Dozens of photos, and in all of them, he's green. Literally green. Head, hands, arms...green. Then there's his flat, inhuman nose and distinctly pointy ears. Eyes so dark they appear completely black.

"I don't understand," I say, meeting her eyes. "This isn't a joke? How can it be anything other than a joke?"

"The world we live in is home to many species of sentient beings. Some of them can pass as human and choose to live in the mainstream. Those that look different have to live in secret, sometimes in towns like Fate's Falls, where they're protected from outside threats."

"This is insane, Ro. Either you're playing the biggest joke of all time on me, or you've wandered past the edge of sanity, and I need to get you off this mountain and into therapy."

"I'm perfectly sane, I promise. And not joking. Not lying." She takes the phone from my trembling hand and stuffs in her pocket, then pulls me into a hug. "Maybe I shouldn't have brought you out here. I could've told you I'd gotten married after the fact. I could've kept everything from you for the rest of your life. If you want to turn around and go back home, I'll understand."

I ease back from her embrace so I can look at her. Inspect her. Ro has never had a good poker face, mostly because she doesn't bother lying. She's as transparent as they come. *Transparent.* I gasp, covering my mouth. "Are invisible people real?"

"Um...maybe? There are none in Fate's Falls, but it's not like we have one of every flavor on the monster menu."

"You call them monsters? That doesn't sound politically correct. Kind of seems like it'd be a derogatory slur."

"Are you saying you believe me?" she asks, ignoring my question about whether it's politically correct to call non-human species monsters. Her delusions are rubbing off on me.

Now *I'm* the one who needs therapy. "I don't know what I believe."

"That's okay. This is a lot to take in." Clasping both my hands, she nods. Gives me a gentle smile. "Do you want to see for yourself? In person. Not pictures on my phone."

"See what? The monsters?" The laugh that bursts from me sounds like a crazed cackle. "Who should we see first? Bigfoot? A werewolf? Your *orc* fiancé?"

"How about a Minotaur?"

My snickering lips snap shut. Eyes wide, my blood flowing hot and cold at the same time, I turn toward the deep voice coming from behind me. "You," I whisper. That's all I can get out while standing face-to-face with a hulking creature who definitely isn't human. But his voice... "Constantine?"

"Yes, Natalie, it's me."

It really is him. But how is it possible? Everything inside me says yes, that's the man from the call. The man I've been thinking about nearly every waking minute for the past two days. The urge to go straight into his arms is overwhelming, as if that's where I belong. Him being a hulking monster with horns and hooves doesn't even bother me. Why doesn't it bother me?

"I think she's going into shock," Ro says, wrapping her arm around my waist firmly. "We should head over to your place so she can lie down."

"Good idea." His amber eyes stay locked with mine. At the end of his wide, flat nose that leans toward being a bull-like snout, his black nostrils flare.

Is he...scenting me? Does he like the way I smell? God, I probably reek after a day full of traveling. Maybe Minotaurs don't find sweat distasteful the way humans do? I have so many questions, the main one being why I'm struggling to stay away from him when all I want is to be wrapped up in his massive arms.

"Come on, Nat. I'll drive your rental car. Constantine

will meet us there. Then we can talk about everything while you're comfortable and safe."

My legs could be steadier and my pulse is still hammering, but I'm not on the verge of fainting. I wriggle free of my cousin's hold and take two tentative steps toward Constantine. "You're really not a man?"

"Not a human man, no."

"But a man," I say, rather than ask. Because there's no question that he's *manly*.

Taller than any human male I've been around. The blue button-up shirt he's wearing looks stretched to its absolute limits across shoulders broader than a football player in pads. His jaw is wide and strong, and his brown skin definitely looks like short, velvety fur. Except on his hands, which are huge. As in, he could crush me with one of them, probably without batting his big, amber eyes. Or, he could do much better things with those big hands. With those long, thick fingers.

A wave of heat washes through me. I very much need to get a grip. "I've been on the go for over ten hours, and I feel grimy from traveling. I could really use a cold drink, a comfortable chair, and a hot shower, in no particular order."

Ro steps to my side, her blue eyes opening wide. "You're okay with...everything? With Constantine being a Minotaur and me marrying an orc? You just flipped a switch and went from borderline hysteria to cool as a cucumber?"

"I definitely don't feel cool." I'm looking at Constantine when I say it. Flirting with him, whether he can read between the lines or not. Maybe I am still a little hysterical.

"But yes, I'm okay," I say, turning my attention to my cousin. "You're healthy and happy. I'm sure I'll probably freak out a little—or maybe a lot—when I'm surrounded by all the different types of non-humans, but at the end of the day, they're still people, right? As long as they're not dangerous, their appearance shouldn't matter."

"Out here," Constantine gestures around us, "there are no guarantees of safety. All creatures are potentially dangerous, monster and human alike. But inside the boundaries of Fate's Falls and other places like it, violence and intentional harm are impossible. The land is protected by very old magic, and only those who are pure of heart and have reason to be there can enter. Everyone within the boundary is safe."

"Monsters and magic and secret towns only selected people can enter..." I push down the burgeoning hyena-like laugh bubbling inside me. "None of this is possible. I'm having the wildest dream of my life."

"You're not dreaming." Ro's hand against mine is warm, solid. "This is all very real, and I'm so happy you're here."

"As am I," Constantine says, his wide, black lips curving upward as he holds my gaze.

Definitely the wildest dream ever. I hope I don't wake up too soon.

Chapter Five

CONSTANTINE

"Maybe I should wake her up and say goodbye before I leave." Outside the closed guest room door, Rosetta taps her toes on the hardwood floor. She told me Natalie fell asleep almost immediately on the short ride from the outpost to my house. No conversation whatsoever. Natalie didn't ask for additional details. She simply got in the passenger seat of her rental car, closed her eyes, and passed out.

Unsurprising, after a long day of traveling and the revelations we dropped on her. She remained asleep after Rosetta parked in my driveway. After I opened the car door. She slept through Rosetta's gentle urgings that they'd arrived at my house. Stayed asleep while I carried her inside. *That* was concerning. Enough so that I called the doctor to pop by and check on her.

All vitals good, the kindly telepath assured us. A quick peek inside Natalie's mind confirmed plenty of brain activity, though the doctor wouldn't disclose what was going through Natalie's unconscious mind. Doctor-patient confidentiality applies, even though Natalie didn't know she was under medical supervision. Dr. Schaefer agreed with exhaustion and acute stress as likely causes for Natalie's current deep-sleep state, advising us to let her rest as long as necessary for her body and brain to catch up.

"The doctor said to let her wake naturally," I remind Rosetta, who has been impatiently waiting it out in my living room for the past two hours. "She said forcing Natalie awake could add additional trauma."

"Then I either go home and you call me as soon as she wakes up, or I can tell Dak to come here and wait with me, even if it's all night. You have that other guest room we can use, right?" She wiggles her ginger eyebrows.

I narrow my gaze at her. "Dak is always welcome in my home, as are you, but surely you can keep your bodies separated for one night."

"Wrong-o. Sex with your mate is like oxygen. Gotta have it."

It has been fifteen years since I engaged in any type of sexual activity. Thinking about physically joining with Natalie has my cock thickening to uncomfortable proportions, which is neither convenient nor appropriate right now. "I'll call you when Natalie is awake."

"You don't think she'll freak out when she comes to in a strange house with a Minotaur for a host, and I'm nowhere to be found?"

"I'm not a stranger, and much more than a host. I'm confident she'll be okay."

Stepping away a stride, Rosetta takes stock of me. "You still think she's your mate."

"I know she is." Sitting idly in the truck earlier was impossible because the pull toward Natalie was so strong. Waiting outside her bedroom is almost a physical struggle.

"Okay, so she's *your* mate. What if she doesn't feel the same way about you? Are you going to be able to stay cool?"

The fur on the back of my neck bristles. "I'm a Minotaur, not an animal. Natalie is safer with me than anywhere on earth. There's literally nothing I wouldn't do to ensure she's safe and happy. My need to protect and care for her is ingrained."

"That's what I wanted to hear," Rosetta says. "And she must trust you too, since she still agreed to stay here, even after she saw that you're not human."

That's because some part of Natalie feels our fated connection. Whether she accepts it—and chooses to stay in Fate's Falls—remains to be seen. But that's not a conversation to have with her cousin.

"Okay, but she may wake up groggy and confused." Rosetta sighs. "Maybe I should just stick around. I'll call Dak and tell him that's my plan."

"Or you could record a short video for her to watch, telling her everything is okay and you'll be back as soon as she needs you."

"Ooh, good idea." Taking her phone from her pocket, Rosetta motions down the hall, toward the living room. "I'll go do that, then head home."

"I would give you a ride, but—"

"No, I'd hate for Nat to wake up completely alone," she says. "Dak will pick me up."

It's wrong to be happy when the front door closes after Rosetta's departure. I should do whatever is necessary to provide comfort for my mate, and having her cousin here would undoubtedly increase her comfort level. But I can't help wanting Natalie all to myself.

After a couple of quick calls to both businesses, letting them know I'll be unavailable for anything less than an extreme emergency, I pour a glass of cold water and head quietly to the guest room door. The sun has disappeared below the treetops, and I don't want Natalie to awaken in total darkness. That's the reason I give myself for opening her bedroom door and entering without consent.

Her scent fills my head the moment I step inside. Light and natural, like fresh rainfall. Whatever travel griminess she felt before falling asleep is unnoticeable and irrelevant to my senses.

I inhale deeply and hold it. Breathing her in this way isn't enough, but it will have to do for now. I tread as lightly as possible, in this moment cursing my choice to forgo carpeting in the guest rooms. Even my most careful steps cause noise; hooves against hardwood will do that.

"Constantine?" Her sleepy voice floats in the darkness.

"It's me. You're in my guest room. I didn't mean to disturb you. I was going to turn on a night-light so didn't wake up surrounded by darkness. Rosetta had to go home, but she'll come back whenever you call her."

"You're not disturbing me, and you can turn on the light. The normal light, not a night-light."

"Do you remember meeting me in the parking lot?" The silence that follows hangs heavy, broken by the sound of my tail swishing against the back of my pants. At least she can't see it. Yet.

"I remember," she says, finally. Softly. "You're a Minotaur, and I'm in a magically protected town full of creatures I'd rather not refer to as monsters, since my cousin is marrying one, and I don't think of you as one."

That's good. Very good. My hand is on the table lamp, but I still don't press the switch. "Before you got in the car with Rosetta, you thought you were dreaming."

"It was a lot of unbelievable information to take in all at once, but I'm okay. Really." Her eyes find mine the instant I turn on the light. Then she smiles, and it brightens the room more than any light source could. "Hi. See? Not freaking out even a little bit."

"I wouldn't blame you if you did, but I'm glad you're feeling more relaxed." I set the water on the bedside table. "Thought you might wake up thirsty."

"Thank you." The blanket Rosetta draped over her falls away as Natalie shifts to a seated position with her back against the headboard. Her delicate chin tips up while she takes a long drink.

Watching her, even in the simple, innocent action of quenching her thirst, stirs the urge to provide for her needs. Food, water, and shelter. Also, her intimate needs. She feels our connection—I know she does. Her scent changed when she heard my voice. Then changed again when our eyes met.

Every breath I take brings more of her sweet arousal to

my nose. I would bury my face between her legs and lick her to completion right now if she consented.

Her eyes go wide at the huff that rumbles from me. "Are you okay?"

"Yes. I control my Minotaur traits to the best of my ability, but nature has its way at times. The bullish huffing, snorting, and tail swishing are involuntary physiological responses. Frightening as they may seem, I promise you'll never be in danger with me, with or without the protection spell over Fate's Falls."

"I'm not scared," she says, rising from the bed. "There's this part of my brain that keeps lighting up with 'this can't be real!' warnings, but it's only a small part, surprisingly."

"I'm very happy to hear it." Standing by the bedside table already put me in close proximity, but now that she's in my personal space, looking up at me, it takes all my willpower not to touch her, especially with her scent filling my nose. Foolishly, I breathe deeper. The effect is as expected—my cock hardens further, straining painfully inside my jeans, and another animalistic huff pushes from my nostrils. "I apologize—"

"Don't. That sound doesn't bother me. Well, it does bother me a little, but not in a negative way." Even in the low lighting, the soft-pink coloring her cheeks is visible. "I'm not turned off by the sound. At all." The rapid fluttering of her eyelashes, the way she pulls her bottom lip between her teeth, then licks her lips afterward... She's turned on. If her other body language wasn't proof enough, her scent is. Her arousal is undeniable; so heady, I can almost taste it.

I haven't been sexually intimate with a human woman

before, but Natalie's biological responses seem well attuned to mine. The temptation to pull her against me is almost too great to resist.

"Are you hungry?" I ask, forcing my mind to places other than the big bed just a few feet away, where I could spread my mate's legs and devour her. "My kitchen is fully stocked, and I'm a passable cook for most things. Or I can take you out instead, if you'd like to get a glimpse of the town. We can order in, pick something up, or I'm sure your cousin would love to have you over. Whatever you prefer."

If her beautiful smile is any indication, Natalie doesn't seem to mind my obvious, overachieving desire to please her. "I'll send Ro a quick message to know I'm awake and not freaking out, but I'd rather stay in this evening, if that's okay with you. I don't expect you to cater to me, though. Pretend I'm not even here."

"That would be impossible, nor is it something I want to do. Catering to you anytime would be my pleasure." Coming on too strong? There's nothing I can do about it if I am. Doesn't matter that she hasn't consented to being my mate. She is mine, and I'm committed to her. I couldn't turn it off if I wanted to.

"In that case, I'm starving. Not picky either. I'll gobble up whatever you put in front of me."

There's no preventing my nostrils from flaring. Not while I'm picturing Natalie on her knees, lapping at my cock. It's too big for her to take into her mouth, but the thought of her exploring every rigid inch, sliding the tip of her tongue over my skin, tasting the milky cum that leaks out...

"Would you mind if I grab a shower first?" Her question snaps me out of my desire-induced imaginings.

"Not at all." A bit of solitary time to pull myself together would be good. "The guest bathroom is directly across the hall, and you'll be the only one using it during your stay, so feel free to make yourself at home. There's plenty of empty space in the cabinets if you want to settle in."

"That's incredibly generous, thank you."

"My home is your home." A statement truer than she's aware, but I'll let her think it's spoken from a place of hospitality. For now. With a nod, I make my way out of her bedroom and head for the entryway, where I left her larger piece of luggage after bringing it in from the car.

While I'm reaching for the suitcase, my phone buzzes in my pocket. A quick check reveals two texts from the evening manager at *The Brew*. Not emergency issues, but questions I should respond to sooner rather than later, so I do.

Once work is out of the way, I collect Natalie's bag and head to her bedroom.

The shower is running behind the closed bathroom door. The guest room door is open wide, so I enter and turn to the right, toward the closet. I set her suitcase beside the dresser, then pivot to leave—exactly as Natalie zips into the room, wearing nothing but a towel.

She shrieks, literally jumping on the spot, clutching the towel tight and causing it to rise higher up her legs—and it was already at the top of them.

"Sorry." I point at the newly deposited luggage. "I heard the shower running and thought it was safe to drop off your large suitcase. I didn't bring it in earlier because I didn't want to risk waking you with any unnecessary noise."

"Oh." That's it. That's all she says while taking stock of me. Batting her eyelashes. Licking her lips.

Knowing I should keep my eyes on her face doesn't mean I do. My gaze drops to the bottom edge of the white terry cloth where it's skimming the apex of her thighs.

She hasn't showered yet and gods help me, I can't resist inhaling. I'm not even trying to hide that I'm breathing her in. The scent of her arousal hasn't waned in the minutes since I left the room. She smells delicious, like the only thing I want to taste for the rest of my life.

Pretty sure my cock has never been harder than it is right now.

"Are you—are we—" The blush on her face deepens. Spreads downward, to the base of her neck, to the swell of cleavage above the towel. "Never mind me, I'm just mentally overloaded and imagining things."

"You're not imagining things."

"How can you say that when you don't know what I was referring to?" Her voice is so soft. Not in a shy way, just beautifully soft.

I grip the back of my neck with one hand, rubbing at the tension there. If I say too much, too soon, I could ruin everything. Maybe irreparably.

"I should get in the shower before I run out all the hot water without getting a drop on me," she says, when I fail to answer her question. "I just came to grab my carry-on bag so I didn't have to put my travel clothes back on." She angles her chin down, then meets my eyes again. "Not sure how I'm going to carry it without losing my towel, though."

My gaze follows hers to the small bag beside the bed. "I'll get it for you. I'll put it outside the bathroom door. You can pull it in after I'm safely out of this part of the house."

"I'm not worried about my safety around you." A laugh bubbles out of her lips and she shakes her head. "That's ridiculous, right? We've talked on the phone a lot the past couple of days, and you're not a *complete* stranger, but..." Again, her gaze travels over me. "You're not human. And you're massive. You have horns on your head and you could probably crush my skull in one of your huge hands. Yet, here I am, not only staying in your home, but standing in front of you, nearly naked. And I'm not even the tiniest bit afraid. What does that say about me?"

"Do you want an honest answer, or casual reassurance?" Best way to know what direction to go is to ask.

"Honest answer."

"You might want to sit," I say, gesturing at the bed.

"I'm visiting a magically protected town filled with monsters and I'm talking to a Minotaur, who I'm interested in, and not in a general curiosity way. At this point, I doubt there's anything you can say that's going to shock me."

We're about to find out. "The ease you feel around me is because you're my mate."

"I'm sorry," she shakes her head, "what did you say?"

"In each Minotaur's lifetime, they have one true, fated mate. You are mine. And while humans aren't bound by the same forces, some do experience the mating bond with species different from their own."

"And you think that's what I'm feeling? You think we," her index finger wags back and forth between us, "two people who've literally just met, are destined to be together?"

"Yes."

"You say that as if you're dead serious."

"Very much alive, and entirely serious, yes."

"Okay, maybe I do need to sit down." One hand on her forehead and the other clutching her towel, she takes a few small steps toward the bed and sits on the edge, unaware that doing so shifts the towel even higher up her hips.

The low lighting in the room casts enough shadow to prevent me from truly seeing between her legs. Thank the gods for that.

Her hand drops from her head to her lap, where she adjusts the towel, maximizing what little shielding it provides. "I really don't know what to say."

"You don't need to say anything, Natalie. Not now, not at any time. I'm here for you, to give you whatever you need. As your mate, I do mean that literally, so never feel shy or awkward to tell me what I can do for you." I wait for her to look up at me. "I'll never pressure you to do or feel anything. I promise you that."

"Okay," she says in that soft voice that makes me want to wrap her in my arms and never let go.

"I'll be in the kitchen whenever you're ready to eat."

There are no defenses shuttering her expression. Her eyes swim with questions and emotions, her lips forming only the faintest smile. "I'll be there soon."

Nodding, I leave her alone in the room, fighting every instinct to do the opposite.

NATALIE

Despite my earlier comment about using all the hot water, it didn't run out during my shower, even though it may have been the longest one I've ever taken. I've always done my best thinking in the shower. Not this time. There's too much crowding my brain. I can't imagine how shriveled I'd be after a shower long enough to sort through everything I've learned since arriving.

My texts to Ro didn't prove helpful, either. She answered my first message immediately, relieved that I'm awake, mentally sound, and sticking around to be her maid of honor. As soon as I changed the subject to Constantine's "you're my fated mate" confession, the conversion changed. Ro sent a big-eyes emoji, followed by a shrug emoji, said we'd talk about it in person tomorrow, then ghosted me.

Talking tomorrow would be fine if I weren't bunking *here*. Sure, I could hide out in my bedroom for the rest of the night. I don't *have* to join him in the kitchen. I'm hungry, but I'm not going to die if I go without eating for one night. If I didn't want to seem totally rude, I could text him and say I'm going to bail on food because I'm exhausted. A reasonable excuse.

That'd only buy me tonight. Tomorrow's Saturday. It's possible he doesn't work on the weekend, or he took the day off to be a good host. What am I going to do if he's out there in the morning? Hole up in my bedroom until Ro finds time to come rescue me? And rescue me from what? Someone who seems perfectly nice and totally accommodating?

Not just nice and accommodating. He's a hunky Minotaur who thinks I'm his fated mate. I may not feel the certainty of a fated-mates bond, but I do feel something. And lots of it. Attraction like I've never experienced—for a man who's not human. I knew there was a spark from the first time we talked on the phone. Our easy connection was a turn-on, even without knowing what he looked like. With each call, each minute spent talking, the connection grew. So did the sparks.

I came here planning to act on those sparks if opportunity presented. To break out of my overthinking mode and have some sexy-times fun during this two-week break from my plodding life.

Well, opportunity has certainly presented. Constantine didn't make a move on me, but the "you're my mate" thing should be an open invitation to get down to it.

Except I don't think it is.

I've never met a human male who'd balk at a quick fling with a predetermined expiration date. No-strings-attached, commitment-free sex is every human man's dream.

But Constantine isn't human. The concept of having one true, fated mate in a lifetime sounds like it has more strings than a marionette. More than a harp. Heck, a marionette playing a harp. And getting caught up in all those strings could make disentangling myself very difficult. Also, it wouldn't be fair to him.

So, decision made. No finding out if Constantine is massive *all over*. My body is going to have to keep on jonesing. I didn't pack my vibrator out of fear I'd be selected for some random luggage inspection. Maybe there's a sex-toy shop in town. That's a question I'm sure Ro will be happy to answer tomorrow. Tonight, I'm going to be a friendly houseguest. It's the least I can do.

Determined to appear more uninterested than I truly feel, I opt for sweatpants, a baggy hoodie, and fuzzy socks. No makeup. Hair in a loose, basic braid. This is the head-to-toe version of granny panties. If I were asked to label this look, I'd call it "man repellent" or "the attraction vaccine."

It's a short trek down the hall to an open-concept kitchen, dining, and living room area. Just like the guest room, everything in here is light, airy, and noticeably over-sized. Monster sized.

Constantine is leaning over a large, granite-topped island, focused on a flat-screen TV on the opposite side of the living room. *The Sports Network.* Apparently, some things are universally "guy," no matter their species.

His rapt attention on the highlight reels gives me a moment to check out this new-to-me backside view of him.

He's still wearing the blue button-up shirt, only now the sleeves are rolled up to his elbows. His forearms are the thickest I've ever seen. There's something about a man with solid arms and rolled-up shirtsleeves. Constantine wins this category by a landslide.

Maybe the clothing here is magically enhanced, too. It must be, because the way his shirt is stretched taut across his unbelievably wide back would be too much strain for normal material and stitching. His long, dark hair lies in neat, shiny waves that end in a tidy line at shoulder-blade level. I shouldn't want to touch it, but tell that to my fingers, twitching at my sides.

There's a subtle V shape to his upper body, but only because his shoulders are so damn wide. He's definitely not thin at the waist. He's deliciously thick. The kind of body that could give protection or the world's best cuddle.

With how snug his jeans fit over what is undoubtedly a solidly muscled butt, the belt he's wearing must be for fashion, not function. And it works. It *all* works. So well, in fact, I'm a heartbeat from sneaking back to my bedroom to make use of my fingers and one of the extra-fluffy pillows while I mentally undress him in private.

Until he turns to face me. "I didn't hear you come in," he says, using the remote to turn off the TV without taking his attention off of me for a split-second. "Feel better after the shower?"

"All cleaned up and fresh. Head to toe and everything in between." I snap my mouth closed. So much for my decision to keep things platonic. I might as well have invited him to inspect my freshness, up close and all over. At least

I'm dressed to un-impress. That'll save me from my uncontrollable, galloping libido.

Leaning back against the island, his gaze sweeps down and up my body. When his eyes lock with mine, he doesn't look unimpressed by my clothing choice or lack of fancying up. Heat swirls in his amber eyes. One of his bullish huffs follows, and this time, he doesn't apologize for it.

Likely because earlier, I all but told him the sound turns me on. Which it did. It does.

"Hungry?" His question could be literal or innuendo.

Either way, my answer is the same. "Starving."

"Let's get you filled up."

Yes, please. Fill me up, Constantine. Fill. Me. Up.

Squeezing my legs together does nothing to relieve the building tug of need. There's no hiding it from him, either.

His big, strong jaw ticks and he draws a deep breath, his nostrils flaring as he undoubtedly catches the scent of my arousal. Tail flicking at his side, he pushes off from the granite and takes a step toward me. *"Natalie."* The deep, rumbling way he says my name sends another ripple straight between my legs.

"Yes?"

"I need you to know that no matter how much I crave you, and even when your body is crying out for me to claim you as my mate, I won't act until you tell me you want me."

I could play coy, tell him I don't know what he's talking about. But we'd both know it to be a lie. "I don't know what's happening to me. I'm a slow cooker at the best of times. I'm attracted to you, but I literally *just* decided it'd be best for us to remain platonic. I'm only here for a couple of weeks and I don't want things to get messy between us.

Then I walked out here, checked you out, and bam, I'm heated to maximum. I'm ready to do all kinds of things I'd never do on a first date. And this isn't even a date; I'm just a guest in your house."

"You know you're much more than that. Attempting to deny or avoid it won't change what fate has in store for us, but we don't have to figure it all out here, now. How about we round up some food, kick back on the couch, relax, and get to know each other. No pressure for more. We can even make a mutual promise that it *won't* turn into more tonight."

"Even if I have a moment of weakness and tell you I want more?"

His dark lips curve into a warm smile that matches the affection in his eyes. "Even then."

"I'd like that. Very much."

"Good," he says, extending one arm toward the living room area while moving toward the kitchen cabinets, where he takes out a serving platter. "Go and get comfortable. I'll bring over a plate."

"Okay." The weight of his attention follows me while I peruse the seating options as if I were Goldilocks. "I don't want to take your favorite spot," I say, looking over at him. "Where do you usually sit?"

To my surprise, he points at one end of the large sectional. "There. But I don't mind switching it up. You might disappear in the divot I've made in that seat cushion, though."

It's so easy to laugh with him. "I'm not *that* small."

"Compared to me, you are." The flare of his nostrils is clear, even from across the room. He's thinking about our size difference in ways that have nothing to do with innocently sitting on the couch.

I know it because I'm thinking about it too. The size of his cock likely matches his big body, and if so, it's huge. He's sure I'm his mate, so sex must be possible. God help me, I want to find out. I have so many questions to ask Ro when I see her tomorrow.

Before the heat between us rises any higher, I turn away, then settle on the best part of any sectional sofa—the inner corner. The earthy-gray velour and pillowy cushions welcome me like an embrace. Fatigue rushes in, not overtaking my arousal entirely, but subduing it. If I close my eyes, I'll be out within seconds.

Not wanting to fall asleep, I shift to a more upright position as Constantine joins me. "Ooh, that looks amazing," I say, my empty stomach making itself known while I attempt to not drool at the contents of the large, wooden serving tray he places beside me.

"It's all yours. Dig in." The couch doesn't shift when he sits, but the depression of the cushion beneath him is definitely visible.

"How much do you weigh?" The question pops out of my mouth as it enters my head. "Sorry! That's too personal a question."

"Between us, there's no such thing. I'll tell you anything and everything you want to know." Again, the heat flickers in his eyes, as if he knows the particular things I was wondering moments ago. "To answer the question you asked, I'm around 180 kilograms. Just shy of 400 pounds."

Three times my weight. He'd crush me if he were on

top. Only, I know he wouldn't, because he'd be careful while fucking me.

Stop thinking about him fucking you, Natalie! Especially while he's sitting right there!

Desperate to be something other than being horny for the horned Minotaur, I focus on the food. A selection of sliced meats and cheeses, crackers and quarter slices of some sort of grainy bread. Assorted cut fruits and raw vegetables. A wedge of pâté with a spreading knife. Little bowls of dip. There are even pickles. Very specific pickles. In fact, everything on the platter looks deliberately selected.

Picking up one of the little green cornichons, I meet his gaze again. The pickle is crisp, tart, and sweet, and I can't help making an *mmm* noise when its flavor bursts in my mouth.

His smile widens. "Good?"

I lick my lips to catch any lingering juice. "Very. Those are my favorite kind of pickles. Did you take notes during our conversation about foods we like and dislike?"

The deep chuckle he makes might as well be his fingers on my clit. "No note-taking required. I remember every detail."

"Your memory is better than mine. I always have a notebook on the go—tabs for work projects, personal stuff, banking, etcetera. On top of that, I have online spreadsheets. Every aspect of my life has to go in a list or a spreadsheet. I can't imagine how much I'd forget if I didn't record it all. I write everything down."

"I hope you left a lot of pages for your Fate's Falls section." He drapes one beefy arm along the back of the couch, the tips of his fingers nearly reaching my shoulder.

The serving tray on the cushion between us prevents me from subtly shifting closer. But I want to. Even though my hoodie would be in the way of skin-on-skin contact, I'm still tingly at the thought of feeling his touch.

I focus on the charcuterie board while I attempt to settle the flutter low in my abdomen. "I think Fate's Falls is going to need its own notebook." Unable to resist, I look at him from beneath the fringe of my eyelashes—and find him staring at me. "Is there a stationery or other store in town that sells pretty notebooks?"

"The notebook has to be pretty?"

"Of course." My body temperature is on the rise again, and it's not from the cozy sweats I'm wearing. The over-sized, nondescript sweats I'm now regretting. I'm not the shapeliest woman around, but my body is decent enough, and I'm kinda wishing he could see it, even though we agreed tonight was just for relaxing and getting to know each other. It wouldn't hurt for him to get to know what I look like when I'm not hidden inside boxy fleece coordinates. Too late now.

"Yes, there's a store. *Fae-vorite Things.* It's downtown, near my coffee shop. Stationery, trinkets, lots of pretty things."

"Is it owned by a non-human?"

He nods. "A fairy named Flora."

"A *fairy?* For real?" Appropriately, or inappropriately, I'm gaping like a fish. "Does she have wings?"

"She does, yes."

"Is she tiny, like a butterfly?"

"No," he says, chuckling softly. "Pixies are small like

that. Fairies are human-sized." He says it all as if it's totally normal. Which it is to him.

"Are there pixies here in Fate's Falls?"

"Several families of them. Quite a few fairies, too."

"Wow, that's...it's all so..." Completely unbelievable. But I'm hearing it from a Minotaur, which makes it as possible as anything. Still, I make a mind-exploding gesture and *kaboom* sound, at which he chuckles again—a sound that makes me smile. "I can't wait to see it all."

"And I can't wait to show you everything."

Warmth washes through me as he looks into my eyes. I should be making these plans with my cousin, not him. I'm here for Ro, not to play *fake dating your alleged Minotaur mate* with Constantine. Except, it wouldn't be fake. And every minute I'm with him makes it feel less alleged.

His smile widens while watching me line up three crackers, then layer each in production-line fashion, until they're perfectly equal mini towers of identical deliciousness. "How much trouble would I be in if I said you're cute?"

"Zero trouble. I never understood women who get bent out of shape by the word cute. Did your last girlfriend have a problem with it?" Now I'm the one whose mouth is going to get them in trouble. "Not that I'm comparing myself to anyone who's had girlfriend status."

"You shouldn't."

It's as if my stomach has a trap door. "Of course not," I say, returning the loaded cracker I'm holding to the tray.

His dark eyebrows draw together, his eyes flaming with intensity as his gaze focuses on the frown tugging my lips downward. He shifts, dropping his arm onto the seat cushions and capturing my hand, where it lies like a dead fish beside the serving tray. "You're my mate, Natalie. Whether you accept what fate chose for us or not, you will always be beyond comparison."

How sad is it that's the most romantic thing anyone's ever said to me? A short time with this man, this Minotaur, is already proof I've dated nothing but duds until now.

Until now. Well, that thought sprang out pretty darn naturally. Is this the beginning of dating Constantine? Am I really going there while I'm here?

Not before we discuss the bigger issue. The one that goes *way* beyond dating.

"How long have you thought I'm your mate?" Attempting to make the moment more casual, I pluck a perfect cherry tomato from the platter and pop it into my mouth.

"I've *known* since I heard your voice. I was fairly certain when I saw your picture. And I've had a sensation in my chest since the first time Rosetta mentioned your name."

The tomato feels like a rock stuck in my throat. I pull my hand from his and beat my fist against my chest, choking the tomato down. "You're kidding about the 'since you heard my name' part."

His gaze stays on my face as he makes a slight headshake. "I'll never lie to you, and I wasn't exaggerating."

"Did Ro know about all this 'mate' stuff when she arranged for me to stay here?"

The dark-brown fur of his face makes blushing impossible, but the set of his mouth seems like an equivalent. "The accommodations were my idea. My offer of guest bedrooms to any of her family who could attend the wedding was sincere, but I was motivated by more than a sense of friendship or goodwill. I wanted *you* here. And no, I didn't tell her you're my mate at the time. Not until after you and I spoke on the phone. When I mentioned it to her after that, she suggested having you stay with a female friend instead of me."

"Why did she change her mind? And then change it back, obviously, since I'm staying here."

"She knows the intensity and permanence of a mate bond. She doesn't want you to get hurt emotionally, but agreed to let you stay at my house because she trusts me to take care of you." He grips the back of his neck and massages it with his big hand. "And because I pleaded with her."

My eyes go wide at that little truth nugget. "You pleaded with her? That's pretty intense, you know. Like, red-flag intense." My heart's thumping a mad beat against my ribs and I swear the temperature in the room just rose five degrees. "Why am I not seeing red flags?"

"Because you feel our mate bond, even if your conscious mind hasn't accepted it yet." What should be a ballsy statement holds no cockiness whatsoever. It doesn't sound irrational, either.

Maybe the magical aspect of this town is affecting my ability to think logically.

"I can tell you're unsettled," he says. "What can I do to ease your mind?"

"I'm not sure that's possible with everything I'm trying to digest." I smooth my hand over my forehead and crown, then slide my fist down my damp braid with a subtle tug, attempting to snap myself out of whatever this is. It doesn't work. The feelings, wild as they are, refuse to be broken. "Okay, explain to me how you're so sure I'm the one."

"I just know. That's how it is with Minotaurs. But that's not the real question you want answered, is it. You want to know why you think I might be right." He's so calm, seemingly at complete ease with this conversation.

"Maybe," I hedge.

Smiling, he offers me his hand, palm up.

I don't hesitate. Placing mine on his is automatic, and I gasp the instant we touch. His hand is warm, firm, soft. The sensation of his fingers closing around mine is electric, but also soothing. My body temperature rises with each second of contact, but it's not just arousal. It's lightness, comfort, excitement, and calm, all at once. More than a physical response. There's a connection.

The amber of his eyes shines brighter than before. "You feel it."

"I feel something, but I already knew I felt something for you. I'm not seeing a 'this is your mate' banner light up in my head. Is that how it is for you?"

The soft lighting casts a shimmer on his dark hair as his body shifts while silently chuckling. "There's no flashing banner. Nothing that literal or tangible."

I give him the single-raised-eyebrow expression. "You're suggesting I should embrace the woo-woo?"

This time, his chuckle is audible. Deep. Super sexy. "If that's the same as relax and be open to possibilities instead of searching for answers, then, yes."

"The woo-woo, like I said. Totally my parents' schtick; it's just never been mine." A smile tugs at my lips, then I exhale and let my eyelids flutter closed. "Okay, here goes."

Taking a deep breath through my nose pulls his scent into my lungs, my head. Earthy, masculine, virile. Warmth flows through me like a gently rippling wave. My skin tingles and a soft, golden glow brightens the insides of my closed eyelids. It's like being immersed in pure energy. And he's there. Not as a picture in my mind, as a presence. I feel like I could touch him...

"You're reaching for me."

"No, I'm not," I say, opening my eyes. "See? I haven't moved."

"You heard that?"

"Of course I did. I had my eyes closed, not my ears."

"You wouldn't have heard it with your ears, Natalie. I didn't say the words out loud."

"Bullshit." I yank my hand back to clap it over my mouth. "Sorry, that's probably offensive because of your, um, heritage. God, saying that probably made it worse."

The deep laugh I remember from our phone conversations rumbles from him. Then he shifts position, moves the serving tray to the coffee table, and gently removes my fingers from my face. "You're fine. No offense taken by any of it. Minotaurs share history with bulls, just as humans do with primates. Would you be offended if I used the term 'apeshit'?"

"No, I'm not a psycho," I say, smiling as tension loosens its grip on my shoulders. Questions about the origins of the other non-human residents in town pop into my head, but I push them aside to make room for more important things. "I distinctly heard you say 'You're reaching for me.' Your voice was crystal clear. You must have said it out loud."

"I didn't. My word to the gods, Natalie."

"Then how? I'm not a mind reader."

"But you are my mate."

"And mates can read each other's minds?"

"Not all mates, but some."

"I don't want anyone knowing what I'm thinking all the time. Have you been reading my mind since I got here?" My face feels hot enough to burst into flames. "Do you know what I'm thinking right now?" I pinch my eyes closed and mentally repeat one word over and over in my head: *Pickles. Pickles. Pickles.*

"Natalie," he says, softly laughing. "I don't know what you're thinking."

"You're sure?" I crack one eyelid open. "You promise?"

"Yes, and yes, one hundred percent. Plus, it was *you* who heard my thought, not the other way around."

"Oh shit, you're right. I don't think I want that kind of power." Still, I can't resist closing my eyes and trying again. Several deep breaths later, all I have is a calmer heart rate. "I don't hear anything now. And it doesn't feel like you're in my head."

He's smiling at me when I open my eyes. "Because I'm not. The first time, I opened myself to you so the mate bond could flow between us. You did more than accept it, you moved into it. Picture opening a door and walking into my mind. It's sort of like that. Though, you hearing my thought was unexpected."

"I'm so sorry. I had no idea I was invading your privacy like that."

"You weren't. I welcomed you there. I always will." Taking my other hand, he gently caresses both while holding my gaze. Sparks skitter through me. Awareness and arousal immediately, then the other sensations return. "Do you feel it now, without closing your eyes?"

"Yes," I whisper, afraid to shatter the feeling by speaking louder. Like before, warmth floods me, wraps around me. And he's there, in my head, like a comforting presence. It's different than before, though. Looking into his eyes makes it extremely intimate. I hope he doesn't let go. Doesn't stop whatever he's doing to make this happen, because I never want this feeling to end.

But it does end, when my phone vibrates in my pocket at the exact moment Constantine's doorbell rings.

Groaning at the inevitable, I slide my hands out of his. "That has to be Ro."

"Did you ask her to come by?" he asks, rising from the couch.

I shake my head while checking my phone. Sure enough, there's a new text from my cousin.

> **Ro:**
> Dak and I are at the door. Thought you might appreciate some backup to reduce the awkwardness. Constantine is a great guy, but I know I should have waited for you to wake up before I took off. Sorry! Here now though! Let us in! Seriously, let us in. I can't wait for you to meet Dak. Don't be scared, okay? He looks like a brute, but I swear, he's really a big green teddy bear.

If she'd sent that message immediately, when I texted her before leaving the bedroom, I would've jumped at the offer. Now, I wish she'd stayed home. Sighing, I return the phone to my pocket and shrug my shoulders while looking up at Constantine. "Better answer the door. I'll go with you." My intention is to tag along behind.

He clearly has other ideas because he takes my hand to help me up, then keeps it.

"We really shouldn't be holding hands when we open the door," I say as we reach the entryway. "I don't want Ro to think we're together."

"She wouldn't disapprove."

"I agree." Stopped at the door, I wiggle my fingers free of his big, warm hand. "But she'd get her hopes up that I've agreed to be your mate, which would mean I'm staying in Fate's Falls."

"You *are* my mate, Natalie. That won't change if you decide to leave after your cousin's wedding."

After what I experienced with him, I really can't argue the "you are my mate" point. I felt it. I liked it. But declaring it is a lot of pressure, especially so fast. Even if I did, I'm not ready to make a decision about the rest of my life. Maybe it's a good thing Ro and her fiancé are here. If Constantine and I had continued down the path we were on, I probably would've agreed to be *his* fiancée before the end of the night. Part of me—a significantly sized part— thinks that would be the best thing ever.

"You didn't hear my thoughts just now, did you?" I ask, when he gently squeezes my hand before releasing it.

"No. I may never be able to, and for it even to be possi- ble, you'd have to open yourself to me—mind, heart, and soul. That can't happen while you're feeling uncertain."

"Wait." Stopping him before he reaches for the door handle, I place my hand on his forearm. The short fur covering his thick muscles is soft beneath my fingers, and I can't resist stroking it. Is the fur on the rest of his big, solid body the same? I want to feel it all. Beneath my hands. Against my naked body. It could be raw physical attraction. I could be having some weird post-traumatic response thing. Or it could be that he really is the one I'm meant to be with.

Nothing about this makes sense. Does it have to, though? It's time I took a page out of my cousin's book, stopped overthinking, and just went with it. Rosetta found true love with a monster. Maybe I will too if I don't close myself off from the possibility. If I open myself to him the way he did with me.

Closing my eyes, I take a deep breath, push my fears and doubts aside, and imagine myself opening a door, hoping he's on the other side. *I'm certain I want you.*

His deep rumble and sharp, bullish huff snap me back to where my mind needs to be. Heat blazes in his eyes. His nostrils flare wildly.

"Did it work with me touching your arm? Could you feel it?"

"Yes, Natalie, I felt it."

I shouldn't expect that he heard the thought I tried pushing toward him, but I'm disappointed that he didn't. "We better answer that," I say, when the doorbell goes off multiple times in succession. Unquestionably my cousin's doing. "The sooner we let Ro in, the sooner we can kick her out."

His body shakes with silent laughter. "I like the way you think."

CONSTANTINE

When I say, "I like the way you think," she's unaware of the depth of those words.

I didn't just feel the connection she initiated. I heard her voice in my head.

I'm certain I want you. She's only certain of the physical aspect right now, but the rest isn't far behind. She believes in the bond. She's just not sure she can accept it.

She will, if I can rein myself in and give her space to get there.

Forcing a genial expression into place, I take a breath, then open the door.

"That took way too long." Rosetta's eyes open wide as her gaze flips between me and Natalie. "Holy shit, were you two *in the middle of something?*"

Natalie's beautiful face flushes bright pink. "We were talking."

"Must've been one *hot* conversation." Rosetta steps inside and pulls Natalie into a hug. "I want all the details tomorrow. Every last one," she whispers against Natalie's ear.

But I hear it, as I'm sure Dak does. Not that his face gives anything away. Orcs are known for their nearly permanent scowl, and Dak is no exception, even in the presence of his beloved mate.

"Get you something to drink?" I ask once he's inside. "Beer? Mead?"

"Water." His dark-eyed gaze slides to Rosetta.

Ah. The pregnancy secret. If I were the betting type, I'd wager Rosetta spills the beans tonight instead of waiting until she shows Natalie the brand-new nursery. "Come on in." I wave them toward the living room. "I'll grab some glasses and a pitcher of ice water. Can I get you something, Natalie?"

"Do you mind if I look at the options?"

"My fridge is your fridge."

Rosetta snorts while leading Dak to the couch, and Natalie follows me into the kitchen. The open layout doesn't give us privacy, but having her near me is a plus just the same.

She inspects the refrigerator's contents while I get a tray, pitcher, and four glasses from an upper cabinet.

"Can't decide what you want?" I ask, standing behind her, close enough that I can breathe her in. Her hair smells like roses, but it's her womanly scent I can't get enough of. I would prefer we come together with our future together resolved, promised to one another. But I will never reject my mate. Whenever and however she wants me, she will have me. Even if I lose her in the end.

"What's in the unmarked can?" She points at one of many beverages in tidy lines on a middle shelf.

"A new beer we're developing at the brewery."

"That's so cool. How's it different from your other beers?"

"It's a Berliner-style Weisse wheat beer, and we've infused it with rose hips to give it a hint of unique, sweet and tarty flavor."

"Wow, I have no idea what any of that means," she says, looking over her shoulder at me. Her wide hazel eyes are so pretty, so clear and sparkly. And her lips, curved up in an easy smile, are the most tempting thing I've ever seen.

My hooves click against the tiled floor as I shift from foot to foot. "It means I sound like one of those annoying craft-beer nerds who talk over people's heads."

The giggle she makes is light and effortless. "Well, you are *literally* talking over my head, because you're so tall. But I didn't take it in a condescending way at all. You sound like someone who's really into the product they're creating. I'm the same way when I'm in a good creative groove."

"I look forward to hearing you talk about your work."

Her happy glow fades. "Well, lately, everything feels more like work than good creativity, so you may have to wait a while."

The urge to tell her we have all the time in the world teeters on the tip of my tongue. Instead, I go with, "Maybe the change of scenery will spark things for you. If not the mountain landscapes, then all the colorful monsters. Like Dak, for example." I tilt my head toward the living room.

She laughs softly, covering her mouth.

If we were alone, I'd take her hand away so I could see the smile she's hiding. Hear her laughter unmuted. We'll get there. I know we will. "Want to be my first non-employee taste tester?" I point at the plain white can again. "If you don't like it, you can dump it and get something else."

"You can't count my opinion because I'm not much of a drinker in general, and definitely not a beer connoisseur, but I'd love to try it."

Leaning in to get the can is an excuse to press my chest to her back. To breathe her in from close up. There's no stopping the huff of breath I make or the wild swishing of my tail. I'm rock-hard for her and I'm sure she feels my cock against her lower back.

She doesn't move away though. The opposite. She leans against me, presses more of her small, delicate body to mine. "Are we still mutually promising nothing will happen between us tonight?"

"We probably should," I say, grazing the shell of her ear as I force myself to do the right thing. "I don't want you to wake up with regrets."

Looking deep into my eyes, a sigh leaves her rosy lips. "I wouldn't regret being with you, but I would regret it if I hurt you."

"You won't." I cup her chin and sweep the pad of my thumb over her soft skin.

"Ahem..." Rosetta calls from the living room. "We're still here, you know. And we're thirsty. Though clearly not as *thirsty* as the two of you..."

Shaking her head, Natalie ducks out from in front of me to look directly at her cousin. "It's good to know that true love and fresh mountain air hasn't changed you."

"Oh, it has," Rosetta counters, pushing up to her knees and hanging over the back of the couch. "But you're never going to know how if you don't stop flirting with the Minotaur and get over here so we can talk."

"Go join them. I'll bring the drinks over."

NATALIE

I should want to throttle Ro for the embarrassing comments, but there's not a lick of anger in me. Despite the fire raging beneath my cheeks, I'm not truly embarrassed either. I can give her a little shit, though. The world wouldn't be right if I didn't.

"Hey, brat," I say, dropping onto the couch, facing her. That's the extent of my giving her shit. As soon as I hug her, all I have are sappy feelings. "I've missed you."

"Ditto, *snore*."

Tears prick in my eyes at the use of our younger-years' nicknames for each other.

Squeezing me tight, Ro whispers, "I know it's selfish, but I hope you fall in love with him and decide to stay."

It wouldn't take much to fall for him. Heck, it's already happening. Which is bonkers and unlike me. I need to slow down. I just don't want to. "Let's focus on making the most of the next couple weeks."

"Right, of course. We're going to have so much fun, I promise." Her nose is rosy and her eyes are glassy when she sits back. Ro's not the weepy type. Her red hair bounces wildly as she shakes her head. Then her usual sassy expression is back. "Introduction time!"

Aside from wrapping his massive arms around her, the orc beside her doesn't react when she climbs onto his lap, wiggling and grinding as she makes herself comfy. Now that I'm truly face-to-face with her fiancé, there's no denying that he is, in fact, an orc.

"Dak, this is Nat. Nat, Dak."

The huge green monster nods at me. "Nice to finally meet you. My Rosetta speaks of you frequently, with love and admiration."

Ro said he's possessive, but the way he says *my Rosetta* seems worshipful. No red flags detected here, either.

I smile, aiming for one that's normal-ish. Not that anything about this is normal. "It's nice to meet you, too. I've heard a lot about you, all very good."

Constantine chokes back a laugh while setting the drinks on the coffee table.

I bite the inside of my cheek because I know he's thinking about the stuff I alluded to during our phone conversation—that Ro likes to tell me spicy stuff about Dak. Now that I know what the guy looks like, it casts those details in a whole new light. Because Dak is huge. Usually, I just listen and giggle when Ro tells her sex tales. Now I have logistical questions.

There's not much space between me and the armrest, but Constantine takes it, rather than sit on the fully available other branch of the L-shaped couch. I scooch over, toward Ro and Dak, but Constantine's hand on my hip halts additional movement.

One of Ro's ginger eyebrows rises and a smile curves

her lips. No mystical mind-meld bond required to know her thoughts. She thinks it's a done deal. That I'm one good Minotaur dicking away from calling Fate's Falls home forever.

She might be right.

Heat from Constantine's body seeps into mine, increasing when he leans forward, his chest pressing tight to my back while reaching for a drink from the table.

I really want that good dicking. To hell with our mutual promise to behave.

His hand is so big, he easily holds the white can and a pilsner glass at the same time. "I wasn't sure which way you wanted it."

"In the can is good."

Ro snickers openly. "You might have to work up to that."

"Ro!" The heat of a thousand suns flares inside me.

Behind me, Constantine's body shakes with amusement.

Even Dak is smiling. Sort of.

Just great. We're all thinking about me getting fucked in the ass by my Minotaur mate.

My Minotaur mate. Not *a* Minotaur, not *the* Minotaur sitting next to me. *My Minotaur mate.* I just mentally claimed Constantine—as my mate.

How would that look in reality, once the euphoria wears off and the rest of the world creeps back in? *Mom, Dad, this is my boyfriend, Constantine, my fated mate, who happens to be a Minotaur.* When I think about saying those things...they don't feel weird. Maybe the magic that safeguards this town really has affected my brainwaves.

The sound of the aluminum tab cracking open jolts me from my thoughts.

"Thank you," I say, accepting the can from Constantine. I take a big mouthful, hoping it'll cool me off and give the others space to start a new line of conversation. Beer isn't my usual drink of choice, but this doesn't taste like ordinary beer. There's no bitterness at all. It's light and creamy, with a distinct fruity tang. Yummy enough for me to take another big swallow immediately.

"Better slow down," Ro teases. "Unless you've been boozing it up a lot since last time we drank together at my farewell night out? The Nat I know is a lightweight."

"I'm just having one." If it gives me a little buzz, that wouldn't be the worst thing. I take another sip, then offer the can to her. "It's one of Constantine's new brews. So good. Honestly, the best beer I've ever tasted. Try it."

"No thanks."

"You'll like it." I squint when she shakes her head. "Worried about cooties from the outside world?" I tease. "I can put some in a glass for you."

"No, I'm good with water."

"You never drink water. You always say it's a waste of your taste buds. This won't be." I'm bordering on asshole territory here, but something's off. Ro's not a lush, but she never shies away from a good time or new experiences. "Come on, try it."

As I jiggle the can, Dak splays his hand over her abdomen. Holy shit. Ho. Lee. Shit.

I never get the chance to make Ro squirm; I've only ever been on the receiving end. This is going to be fun. I crank the drama dial high, pushing my bottom lip out in a pout. "I came *all* the way across the country for you, and you won't even take a sip of this delicious beer I'm sure you'll like? You *have* changed." I fake a sniffle for extra effect.

"Oh shit, you figured it out, didn't you?"

"Figured what out?" I ask, exaggeratedly fluttering my eyelashes.

Ro rolls her eyes, then the biggest smile I've ever seen spreads across her face. "That I'm pregnant, dork!"

The two of us squeal in unison, like we used to do as kids. As teenagers. As young women stepping into adulthood for the first time.

"Oh my god, Ro!"

Constantine grabs the can from my hand as if we planned the move. Then I'm hugging my cousin, squeezing her tight. But not too tight, because her "I swear, he's really a big green teddy bear" fiancé is giving me major stink-eye over her shoulder. Or at least I think he is. With his dark eyes and perpetual scowl, it's hard to be sure. But it feels like a stink-eye occasion for some reason.

"Role reversal. You're the brat now," she says, smacking my shoulder after releasing me. "I had a whole amazing plan for telling you about the baby. Tomorrow, at my house, in the beautiful nursery Dak busted his ass to finish, solely for that reason." She cranks around to face him, cupping his green jaw and kissing him, protruding tusk teeth and all. "Sorry, baby. I'll make it up to you."

Baby? She calls her hulking, monster fiancé *baby?*

And he doesn't seem to mind. Not that I'd be able to tell if he did.

She plants a deeper kiss on him, one that has him

pulling her back onto his lap, where he not-so-subtly rocks her back and forth while they make out as if Constantine and I aren't sitting right here.

Okay, then...

I inch backward until I connect with Constantine, but pervy me can't stop staring at the extreme PDA in front of me. Angling my head up and back against his chest, I whisper, "Should we leave the room?"

He tips his face down, close to mine. "If we do, they'll have sex on my couch, and that's a mess I'd rather not have to clean up."

"I heard that," Ro says, breaking her lip-lock to look at us and stick out her tongue. She really hasn't changed since moving here. Falling in love with a monster and getting pregnant with his baby don't seem to have mellowed her sass at all. "Since you look plenty comfortable and not trau-matized *at all*," she makes a circular swirling motion toward us, "Dak and I are going to head home."

"But you just got here." There's not a lot of life in my protest, I admit.

Ro's snicker tells me our year apart hasn't diminished her ability to read between the lines with me. "We'll have some bestie time tomorrow; it's all arranged. Constantine's going to take you to his coffee place at nine-thirty, and we're meeting up with Dela, another human who lives here now. She's a sweetheart, you're going to love her. From there, we'll do a bit of shopping while you check out everything Fate's Falls has to offer." One eyebrow rises over mischievously twinkling eyes. "Well, *almost* everything."

"You're still a brat," I say, rolling my eyes at her while pushing up from the couch.

She takes my hand and lets me pull her to her feet, then bear-hugs me. "You wouldn't want me any other way."

It's true. If Ro didn't tug me out of my comfort zone, I'd probably never leave it. Right now, that means I'd still be back in my little apartment, alone and lonely as I plod through life, wishing for things I'd never find there.

Things I've already found here.

Generic conversation is passed around as we all head for the front door. One more hug from Ro, then she and Dak are on their way home, likely to fuck each other's brains out. If they can't keep it under control sitting next to us on the couch, I can't imagine what they're like in private.

The energy in Constantine's house changes as soon as he locks the door behind them. All the sexual tension from earlier comes rushing back the moment we're alone.

"I'm going to clean up the food and drinks," I say, trying to focus on anything other than wanting to climb him like a tree.

He shakes his head. "I'll take care of that later. Can I get you anything? Another drink, different food?"

Your body rubbing up against mine would be good...

"No." I shake my head emphatically, probably looking like a weirdo in the process. "I think I'm ready for bed. Alone," I add, heat rushing to my face and between my legs. "Even though I'm tempted to ask you to break your promise that nothing will happen between us tonight."

"I'm not sure I could deny you if you did."

The pull between us is magnetic. I move closer, stopping with little more than a hairsbreadth separating us. "I'm not sure I can deny myself." Unable to resist, I place my hands on his big chest. "I swear I'm never like this," I say, looking up at his non-human face while sliding my palms over every inch of his shirt-covered torso. "I don't do stuff with someone I just met. I've never been someone to rush into things. But with you, I just want to jump in and do it all."

A rough huff of breath accompanies a deep rumble in his chest. "Doing it all will take time."

"It's not *that* late…" Am I doing this? Going for it? I think I am. "And I'm not tired anymore."

"Not time as in hours." He cups my waist and pulls me tight against him, so my soft body molds around the very large, hard bulge in his jeans. "Time meaning preparation."

Oh. "But it's possible, right?" I bite my lip, fighting the urge to reach down and touch him *there*. "A Minotaur and human can…fit together?"

"I've never been intimate with a human, but there are many recorded couplings."

"Recorded? As in cross-species porn videos?"

His body rocks with deep, low laughter. "I should have said 'documented,' as I was referring to historical records of mated couples."

I groan, pressing my forehead against his chest to avoid looking him in the eye.

One of his large hands cups my chin and tips my head up. The smile is still on his face, but it's less amusement, more seductive. It matches the heat in his gaze. "But there are videos of the type you mentioned."

"Oh," I say, another wave of heat rolling through me. "Have you watched any?"

He gives a single nod. "Only after discovering I have a human mate."

"Curiosity about the fitting thing?"

Another nod. "Are you curious?"

"Very. Where can I see them?"

"There are some websites you won't be able to access unless your device has our enhanced settings and protections. You can use my computer if you'd like to—"

"Yes," I say, cutting him off. My face couldn't be any hotter than it is right now. The rest of my body matches, too. "I know porn isn't reality, but I need to see how it'd work if we—*have sex*."

Nostrils flaring, he steps back. "I'll get my laptop and bring it your room so you can have privacy."

"Okay." I nearly stumble while walking away. Not from the beer I drank, the lightheadedness is purely adrenaline. I'm about to watch monster porn on my Minotaur mate's computer, so I know what to expect when we have sex. Who am I and what is this reality I'm suddenly part of?

In my bedroom, I don't know what to do with myself while waiting for him. Should I wait at the door? Sit on the bed? *Lie* on the bed, patting the mattress? I glance down at the outfit I'm wearing. Definitely not the third option. This isn't a seduction scene; it's research. Really freaking sexy research.

I nearly jump out of my skin when he raps on the doorframe.

"Didn't mean to startle you," he says, offering the laptop across the threshold. "There's no password, and it's queued up if you want to watch one of the more romantic videos. If you change your mind, you're welcome to use the computer for whatever you want. You can look at all your regular human internet stuff, too, and nobody outside of Fate's Falls will be able to track your activity."

"Because of the magic?"

He nods. Winks. "Best firewall there is."

"I'm not sure if I'll watch the video." Awareness sizzles through me when our fingers brush while I take the laptop from his hand. Who am I kidding—I'm watching it the second I'm behind a closed door. The way his eyes are twinkling, he totally knows it. "I'll see you in the morning?"

"Anytime you want, Natalie. My room's at the other end of the hall if you need anything."

If I open my mouth to speak, who knows what'll come out. What I'll tell him I *need*. Instead, I nod and smile. Hope he can't tell how turned on I am. How eager I am to see what a Minotaur cock looks like, so I know what's in store for my ghost town of a pussy.

Chapter Eight

CONSTANTINE

Sleep may not be possible tonight.

My mate felt our bond, didn't deny it, and openly voiced her sexual attraction and the difficulty she's having containing it. Down the hall, she's watching video of a male Minotaur fucking a human woman. And she's enjoying it.

I probably should have been forthcoming about my Minotaur senses. Told her that my hearing and olfactory receptors far exceed those of humans.

Even with two closed doors and many meters between us, I heard the video when she pressed the *play* button, heard her gasp of embarrassment, and the sharp stabbing at the keyboard as she muted the volume. Now I can hear her soft moans. I can smell her heightened arousal.

I couldn't fall asleep now if my life depended on it.

Not with my cock harder than it has ever been, throbbing with need for my mate. I don't dare take myself in hand. Natalie wouldn't require heightened senses to hear me. Minotaurs are not quiet when sexually engaged. That's all I need—for Natalie to knock on my bedroom door because she hears me lowing while I relieve the pressure in my heavy balls.

Closing my eyes only serves to heighten my other senses. Lying on my back, I grab fistfuls of bedsheets as the sound and scent of her climax—the third one—fill my head. A cold shower won't help, but I'll take one anyway. The pounding water may drown out the sound of things I crave to experience up close.

Light tapping on the door stops me in my tracks as I'm crossing to the en suite bathroom. I glance at my raging erection, then at the door. There's no way to hide my physical state. I could pretend I didn't hear the knock, but I did tell her I'd be available if she needs something.

I pull on a bathrobe and cinch the belt tight, restraining my cock in an upward position against my body, then open the door.

"I watched the video," she says before I can ask what she needs.

My gaze drops from her glassy eyes and flushed cheeks. The baggy sweats from earlier are gone, replaced by a pale-pink bathrobe that ends above her knees and molds to her body. The hard points of her nipples strain against the thin material, proof that she's not wearing a bra underneath.

Like a glutton for punishment, I inhale deeply, unable to prevent the animalistic huff of breath from rumbling out of me when her scent fills my nose. I should apologize, but I can't. Holding back from touching her takes every resource I possess.

"I—" Her gaze trails down from my face, following the front edge of my robe to the V where my furry chest is exposed, then lower, to the bulge of my cock behind the ties. "I don't think I'll be able to have sex with you." Her eyes flick back to mine. "Not if your... *equipment* is the same size as the Minotaur in that video."

It's bigger. But I'm not about to tell her that and send her running. "I'll never pressure you to do something you're not interested in."

"But I *am* interested." The tip of her pink tongue darts out to moisten her lips. "I'm very interested. In you. Like, uncontrollably interested. Going-out-of-my-mind interested. Is there something about this town that causes that reaction in human women? Because, obviously, my cousin is experiencing the same thing, after I watched her practically going at it with Dak, right in front of us."

"It's not the town, it's the mate bond."

"Theirs?" she asks, and I nod. "And... ours?"

"Yes. And ours."

"The mate bond is why I'm standing at your bedroom door when I *know* I should have stayed in my room? Why I feel like we've known each other forever, even though we've just barely met?"

"That's how it is with mates, yes."

"So... there's nothing I can do to stop what's happening, to control these feelings and urges I'm having for you? Fate decided we're supposed to get together, so it's inevitable?"

Getting everything I want might be as simple as telling

one small lie she'd never have to know about. But she would never be truly mine that way. "There is a way for you to be rid of the feelings you're experiencing." Tightness twists in my chest, in my gut, making it difficult to say what needs to be said. "You can reject me."

"It's that simple? Just say I'm not interested, and it all goes away?"

"A little more formally than that, but yes, it'd be that simple for you."

"What about you?"

I shake my head. "If you reject me as your mate, the bond is broken for you, not for me."

Her delicate eyebrows draw together. "But you could reject me, too, right? Then we'd both be free to fall in love with whoever we choose."

"I assume you, as a human, would have that option. If our bond is broken, I could have sex with others, but I would never find another mate. I'd never love someone. Fate gives each Minotaur one person for that."

"You're saying if I reject you as my mate, you lose any chance at love?" The air goes out of her in a *whoosh* when I nod. "If I don't want to commit to a fated mate bond I didn't know existed until today, I'm robbing you of your only opportunity at a happily ever after? That's a huge amount of pressure."

"Don't let my feelings or future affect your decision." I tuck a strand of hair that's worked free of her braid behind her ear, then trail my fingers along her cheek. "I want your happiness more than my own."

"Let me guess," she scrunches her nose, "that's because of the mate thing."

Even with everything hanging in the balance, and her obvious frustration, I feel light enough to smile. "Yes, but also because I'm a pretty decent man."

"You are pretty," she says, laughing softly. "And from what I've heard and seen so far, decent, too."

"Nobody's ever called me pretty before." I tilt my head. "Well, aside from your cousin, but she only said it to piss me off."

Once again, she pinches her eyebrows together. "I meant it as a compliment."

"And that's how I took it." Touching her after the heavy conversation might be pushing it, but I do it anyway, capturing one of her hands and weaving her fingers between mine.

"What if, after you get to know me better, you realize I'm going to drive you crazy with my grab bag of quirks? Because I've got lots. Would you reject me then?"

"Of all possible mates, fate chose you for me. Made me wait fifteen years for you. I already know you're exactly right for me. I promise you, now and always, I will never reject you."

"Then...would you walk me to my room and kiss me goodnight?"

"It would be my honor and pleasure." Shifting my hand to the small of her back, I guide her down the darkened hall, my cock hardening more with each moment I feel her warmth beneath my palm.

At her bedroom door, she faces me and gently curls her hands around the front edges of my robe. "I like you." Color rises on her cheeks as she slips her fingers beneath the fabric and through the short fur of my chest. "And you know I'm attracted to you."

"Both good things and feelings I share," I say, wrapping my arms around her snugly enough for my cock to make itself known against her belly.

"But everything about this is new to me, and it's all happening so fast. I have a lot to think about before I do something that will permanently affect both our futures."

"I understand. And I'm grateful you're willing to take some time before you decide."

"Is there a line I should know about? A limit to how far things can go between us before the mate bond kicks in officially? If we kiss, are we sealing it? Or if we have sex, if that's even possible, is that what makes it final? I would hate to hurt you later because I got caught up in the heat of the moment, and unknowingly committed to more than I'm aware of."

Whether she's ready to admit it yet or not, she is my perfect one. She's willing to sacrifice pleasures she obviously wants if that pleasure would make *my* future painful. Fate chose well.

"Whether we enjoy each other sexually or never share a kiss, we're already mates. We will be until the end of our lives, unless you break your bond."

Her lips part as she blinks up at me. "Then...kiss me. Not a goodnight kiss. The kiss you'd give me if it were the only kiss we'd ever share."

Desire to please my mate roars to life inside me. Sliding my hands up her back, I find the end of her braid and tug the elastic away. Her hair is damp around my fingers as I thread my fingers through it and let it sift free. "Beautiful." I lean down and press my nose to her crown, breathing in the floral scent of her shampoo. "Lovely, but nothing compares to the scent of your arousal."

A soft gasp rises between us, then a sharper one when I wrap her long locks around my hand and gently tug, causing her head to tip back.

"Are you sure you want me to kiss you as if I only have one chance?"

"Yes," she whispers. "God, yes."

"Then I hope you aren't in a hurry to sleep." Angling above her, I inhale the scent of her skin, of her breath, then seal my wide mouth to her smaller, softer one.

She opens for me instantly, welcoming my tongue with a moan that drives me to kiss her deeper, harder. The tip of her small tongue touches mine, igniting sparks that race straight to my cock. Soft, breathy sounds rise to my ears like sweet, sexy music. And the taste of her—gods, the taste of her. One kiss will never be enough.

Inside my robe, her hands glide over my chest, up to my shoulders, then down to my abdomen, as far as our position allows. Close enough to feel the head of my cock where it protrudes above the level of the robe's belt.

She gasps again, whispering against my mouth, "I know I told you to kiss me, but can I see you?"

"You can have whatever you want, Natalie. In all ways, for all things, I'm yours." Releasing her hair, I ease back to give her full access to do whatever she wishes.

Looking up at me with glassy eyes, she unties my robe and slides it off my shoulders. "I—" Whatever words she thought to say morph into a choked gurgling sound as her gaze travels over my naked form. "You're huge. Everywhere. So, so, *huge*."

Pride at impressing my mate brings my bullish nature to the forefront. A loud, assertive huff pushes from me, my hooves scrape against the floor, and my tail swishes like a flag in the wind. And my cock—it juts tall and hard, the wide, bulbous head shiny from the milky precum beading out.

I step closer, cup her face in one hand while cradling the back of her head with the other. Then I taste her lips again, teasing them apart with my tongue.

She melts beneath me, her body pressing to mine as her hands explore my fur-covered muscles, my waist, then, finally, my cock. Her fingers curve around the shaft—both hands, the tips barely meeting.

I groan into her mouth as she strokes me, and when she drags one fingertip through my leaking slit, the groan turns into a near-feral growl. I break our kiss, capture her tiny wrist, and draw her hand up between us. "Taste," I say, guiding her finger to her lips.

Her tongue peeks out first, tentatively obeying. Her eyes open wide, then she sucks her fingertip between her lips, humming until her finger pops free. "It's sweet." A laugh bubbles up from her glistening lips. "If all men tasted like you, there'd be no more complaints about not getting enough blowjobs." She lowers her gaze to my cock. "Though I don't think giving you one is within the realm of possibility for me."

I tip her chin up so our eyes meet. "There are many other ways we can enjoy each other."

Holding my gaze, she releases the tie at her waist, slides the robe off, then brings my hands to her bared skin. "Show me."

Chapter Nine

NATALIE

I've never been a sexual initiator. Or sexually adventurous. Or quick to engage in any kind of intimate activity. I've absolutely never done things the first night I was with someone. And it goes without saying that I've never been with a Minotaur.

If all of this were a dream, it would be the wildest, best dream anyone could have. But it's real. I'm naked with Constantine and our kiss is about to become a whole lot more.

"Natalie." The way he says my name sends warmth to every cell of my being. "So beautiful, my perfect one." He slides one thick, powerful arm around my back and pulls me flush against him, then dips down to kiss me again. His mouth is much bigger than mine, but our lips fit together as if they were meant to.

I run my hands all over him, sparks skittering through me as the short fur covering most of his body tickles my palms, my breasts, and every other bare, sensitive part of me. I'm being thoroughly and properly kissed by a monster. His tongue is long and broad and should feel like too much when it strokes into my mouth, but it's perfect. Warm and tickly and firm. Each kiss, each sweep of his tongue, tightens the longing tug between my legs. The achy emptiness I'm desperate for him to fill.

But that cock... holy hell, that cock. I could barely circle it with both hands. And it's so freaking long. There's no way it can fit inside me. But I want it to. God, I want it to.

The couple in that video had no problem fucking. That Minotaur wasn't as thick as Constantine, but he was still huge, and the woman didn't just take it—she took it like, well, like a porn star.

"That video," I say, breaking our kiss. "The couple, do you think they're bonded, or just having sex?"

"They're mated."

I pull back a little more so I can see Constantine's face. "How do you know?"

"Their bio was in the video description."

God, he's cute. Massive and sexy, yes, but cute. "You're probably the only creature on the face of the earth who reads the video description on a porn site." I squeak when he scoops me up into his arms. The position puts his arm directly under my ass, his fur teasing between my legs as he strides to the bed.

I expect him to lay me out, but instead, he sits me on the edge, parts my thighs, then drops to his knees between them. I can't even remember the last time a man voluntarily went downtown. I do know it wasn't in a fully lit room. And never like this, with me sitting up, watching. Yet I'm not the teensiest bit self-conscious. When he leans in, takes a deep breath, then one of his bullish huffs wafts over the place I want his mouth, I feel desired more than I ever have before.

Fire blazes in his amber eyes as he takes my hands and brings them to his horns. "Grip me hard and pull me in. Ride your bull's face until you come."

Oh. God. He's *so* dirty. And it works. It *so* works.

His horns are hard and coarse against my hands. I tighten my grip pull his face closer to my pussy. Eyes on me, he drags that wide black tongue across my sensitive pink flesh. I gasp at the immediate rush of need he stokes, pulling him tighter against me to get more. And he gives it.

My head falls back as his tongue burrows inside me, wiggling and thrusting, pressing against places that make me moan and squirm. Holding his horns, I rock against his face to take his tongue deeper, to feel his nose press against my clit. Squelching wetness and ravenous slurping fill my ears and I almost come from the deliciously dirty sound of being eaten out by my Minotaur mate.

He's my mate, and god, I am *so* his.

Would it work this way? The bond? Eyes closed, I open my mind to him. Clear away everything except him and me and the way he's making me feel. Warmth like before flows through me, and then he's there, in my mind.

Suck my clit.

His mouth rumbles against my pussy, then his tongue slides up to my clit, circling, circling, before he sucks it hard enough to send me over.

Moans and squeals and babbled curses fly out of me as I jerk and writhe against his face, coming for what feels like forever. When I can't take any more, I let go of his horns, but he doesn't stop. He keeps suckling. Circling. Nuzzling. Until I'm coming again, this time long and gently, like a rippling wave.

My perfect one.

The words in my mind are as clear as if he spoke them aloud, and I snap my eyes open to find him watching me. He lavishes one last, long lick before rising between my legs.

"I heard you again," I whisper. Zero shyness about what we just did, but my heart is racing because of hearing a few words through our bond. A connection *I* initiated—while his face was buried in my pussy.

"I heard you too."

"I kind of figured, since you immediately did what I thought." My face must be the color of a fire engine. "Sorry that the first thought of mine you heard was a sex command."

His deep chuckle makes all his muscles dance. His cock too. "I welcome your sex commands anytime, mental or spoken aloud, but that wasn't the first time I heard your voice in my mind. Before we answered the door earlier, you thought, *I'm certain I want you.*"

"I didn't think you heard that. You didn't tell me."

"Your cousin was trying to beat the door down at the time, then we never circled back to it." The way he looks at me while stroking my face makes my heart want to beat its way right out of my chest.

"This is all so surreal. I can't believe any of it is really happening."

"Do you wish it wasn't?"

"I have no regrets." I smile up at him, happiness blooming inside me like the most beautiful flower. No more denial. I want this. I want him, even though I have no idea how to make it work, long term. That's something to worry about another day. "Is that normal, hearing your mate's thoughts so early and easily?"

"Honestly, it's unexpected, with you being human. But it would seem it's normal for us, and I welcome it."

"It freaked me out the first time, but... I like it."

"That makes me very happy," he says, dipping down to kiss me.

Tasting myself on his lips and tongue strikes a match inside me. "Keep kissing me," I say. "I want to try again, like this." It's trickier this way, but as we find our kissing rhythm, I relax and open the door in my mind.

He's right there, his mental presence as big and warm and addictive as his physical being.

Can you hear me? I want to taste you again. Feed me your cum.

The kiss ends with his rough rumble vibrating through me. Heated gaze locked with mine, he guides both my hands to his cock. "Stroke me. Milk me so I can feed it to you."

So very dirty.

Giving a two-handed hand job is a first, but my inexperience and irregular strokes don't seem to turn him off. His massive, dark cock responds to my ministrations, quickly pulsing beneath my palms. I glance down, my mouth watering at the steady beads of precum leaking with each upward stroke.

"Open your pretty mouth for me," he says in a husky voice, then, "Gods, you're perfect," when I do exactly what he wants.

Because I want it too. I asked for it. Through our bond.

"Squeeze harder. As hard as you can, you won't hurt me." He makes a sexy-as-hell bullish snort when I double-down on the stroking. Behind him, his tail swishes wildly from side-to-side. His hooves stomp at the floor—once, twice. Then his mouth forms an oval and he lows, long and loud, while warmth coats my fingers and rolls down my hands.

Holding my gaze, he reaches down, then brings two loaded fingers to my mouth and spoons the thick, milky substance into my mouth. Tapping my chin, he watches me close my mouth and swallow.

This is definitely the dirtiest thing I've ever done, but it just feels right. "I want more," I say, holding my mouth open like a baby bird. I swallow the next mouthful as quickly as the first, then lie back on the bed, lightheaded and spinny, licking the cum off of my hands like a kid would with cake batter after scraping the mixing bowl. "What did you mean when you said 'doing it all' would require preparation? What kind of preparation?"

The bed shifts as he settles alongside me, propped on one arm and looking down at my face. "Stretching exercises."

"Like yoga?"

"No," he says, smiling. "Not like yoga."

I gasp as he touches between my legs, at the thickness of his single finger sliding inside me. *Ohhh... stretching exercises.* For my vagina. I hum when he withdraws, using my slickness to lubricate my clit while he teases it. "This is my kind of exercise."

"This isn't the stretching part, just the warmup."

"Never skip the warmup." Giggling at my own wittiness, I slide my hand down his body. His cock is still hard, or hard again, I don't know which, and sticky with cum. Wasted cum. "Why does this taste so good?" I ask, lifting my hand toward my mouth.

He catches my wrist before I can lick my fingers. "Because you're my mate. And I love watching you enjoy the taste of me, but Minotaur semen is good for other things, too."

"Making baby Minotaurs? I'm on the birth control pill to regulate my periods, so we don't have to worry about that."

The rumble he makes and the emotions swirling in his eyes tell me he wouldn't be worried at all if he got me pregnant. That he'd like it.

And that turns me on almost as much as everything else about him. "Aside from breeding, what else is Minotaur semen good for?" Saying the word *breeding* makes me desperate to feel him inside me. Desperate to come again.

"It's known to heighten sensation." He guides my fingers between my legs. "Try it here."

Apparently, I've become an obedient little naughty human, because I get busy on my clit without having to be convinced, and I have never, ever, masturbated with an audience. Not even in front of a mirror. But I don't even blink about doing it in front of Constantine. And that sensation-heightening thing? Oh yes. I'm already so close, I'm not sure I can stop. "Touch me again..."

On his side, he presses against me, his deep rumble sending vibrations rippling through me. His hard cock lies heavy across my legs, its fat tip leaking milky white cum that runs down the inside of my thigh. "Gods, Natalie, you're so fucking beautiful," he says, sliding one thick finger inside me again. His single finger is nearly as big as a human cock—but not nearly as big as *his* cock.

"One more," I pant, rolling my fingers back and forth over my clit, my gaze lowering to his hand between my legs as he withdraws, coats two fingers in pearly precum, then enters me again. The fullness forces my eyelids to flutter closed. Whatever it is about his semen that's a sensation enhancer goes to work immediately, setting me ablaze with the need to come. Broken words and breathy panting are the extent of my communication as he moves those two huge fingers deep inside me, tapping them against a place no man or vibrator has ever found. I cry out, high-pitched, coming in a never-ending hot wave of pleasure.

When my body raises the white flag and I'm boneless and breathless, he slides his fingers from my pussy, then sucks them into his mouth. Growling. Nostrils flaring. *"Natalie,"* he warns when I curl my hand over his huge cock and slide it along the shaft.

"I want you."

Heat flares in his amber eyes. "Your pussy isn't ready for my cock."

"Then make it ready." At the end of a stroke, I gather a generous amount of precum and rub it between my legs. "That will help, right?"

"Yes, it will help, but—" A rough, bullish huff pushes

cuts off his words as I tug his hand to my pussy again, positioning three of his thick fingers at my entrance.

"Get me ready."

"Even if you can take all four of my fingers tonight, I won't fuck you afterward, you'll need time to recover."

"Four?" The word squeaks out of me.

Raising his hand, he groups his fingers together, showing me the size of them, then lowers his hand, placing it alongside his cock.

Oh god. His cock is...bigger.

"I..." That's never going to fit inside me. I want it to, but there's just no way.

"It will fit."

"You heard my thoughts?"

"Not this time," he says, smiling, gently cupping my face. "But they're written all over your beautiful, terrified face."

"Not terrified, just..." I bite my lip, then sigh. "Okay, mildly terrified, because that thing is massive."

The upturn of his thin black lips and the bullish huff he makes are undeniably male pride. Then his expression gentles, and he draws me against him, my back to his front, that giant battering ram of a cock nestled between us. "I will happily spend my life pleasuring you with my tongue and fingers only."

I tilt my head to see his face. "You'd be okay with never having actual sex? For the rest of your life?"

"I would be happy just to be with you, Natalie, with or without sex of any kind."

It'd be an unbelievable claim from any human man I've

ever met. Given Constantine's obvious sexuality and prowess, it should be unbelievable for him, too.

My heart tells me it's true.

"You don't have to go," I say, when he presses a kiss to my hair, loosens the arm wrapped around me, and he begins to move away. "I mean... I don't expect you to stay. But you can. If you want to."

"I want to." Despite his big, bulky physique, he shifts us between the sheets smoothly, almost effortlessly. He ensures my head is on one of the soft, cool pillows, my hair tucked neatly behind my shoulders. Then his big arm wraps around me again, and he snuggles in tight behind me, cradling me with his soft, furry body. "Are you comfortable?"

Covering his hand with mine, I close my eyes and open my mind to him. *More than ever in my life.*

His deep rumble vibrates against me, an unspoken confirmation that he heard my answer through our mate bond. "Sleep well, my perfect one."

Chapter Ten

NATALIE

"I'm sorry Rosetta is late," I say to Dela, glancing at the wall clock for what has to be the tenth time since she joined me at my table in Constantine's cozy-yet-hip coffee shop—right on time, which was half an hour ago. "You don't have to stay. I'm sure you'd rather not hang out in your workplace on your day off."

Dela, a semi-new-to-town human who is one of Constantine's full-time weekday employees here at *The Brew*, smiles while shaking her head. "I'm happy to wait. Constantine is a great boss, and my coworkers and the customers are so nice, being here never really feels like work. I often come in for coffee on the weekends."

"Ask her if that has anything to do with hoping to catch a glimpse of a certain red hell demon she has the hots for," a woman's voice says from behind me, then its owner turns one chair at the neighboring table toward us and sits.

Based on the full-face glowing blush on Dela's face, that comment hit the bullseye.

"Wait a sec," I say, looking back and forth between them. "There are hell demons here?"

"A few," the woman who's sort of sitting with us says, a playful smile curving her full, plum lips. "But the one Dela has a crush on won't be here today, because he knows she's not working."

Dela rolls her eyes, but there's a noticeable uptick in her expression. "He comes in for the coffee, Shay. Not because of me."

"You are in such denial." The woman's dark curly hair bounces with her light laughter, then she turns her attention to me. "I'm Shay, Dela's coworker slash self-appointed life coach."

"Shay's being gracious. It'd be more accurate to say I forced her into the position because I constantly need help." Warmth and sincerity fill Dela's voice, matched by an expression of genuine affection as she smiles at Shay. "I basically made Shay adopt me when I moved to town seven months ago."

"Girl, I'm only six years older than you." Shay crosses one high-booted leg over the other. "But I love you like a sister, and because of that, I get to tease you like one, too."

"You two sound a lot like Rosetta and me. We're cousins, but we've always been more like sisters. I'm Natalie, by the way." I offer my hand to shake, but Shay salutes me with her takeout cup instead.

"I make a point not to touch people," she says. "Everyone, not just you. It's a me thing." Her green-eyed gaze appraises me. "You and Rosetta being close explains how easily you're handling all the monster stuff." She tilts her head toward a naga and a goblin having coffee a couple tables over.

"Oh, I didn't know anything about the existence of non-humans until yesterday afternoon, when I got here, and met Constantine." Just saying his name stirs warmth in my chest. Between my legs. After being wrapped up in his arms all night, I woke up alone in bed this morning, my stomach growling at the aroma of the breakfast he was cooking in the kitchen. We kissed good morning—long enough that he had to remake the eggs that shriveled in the frying pan—then ate together like an old married couple. If old married couples have chemistry that feels like magnets being pulled together, that is. If I didn't have plans to meet Ro, I'm pretty sure Constantine and I would be naked in bed right now, working on those *stretching* exercises.

"Earth to Nat. You in there?" Ro snaps her fingers in front of my face.

My cheeks heat to inferno temperatures at the realization I've been caught daydreaming. "Oh good, you're finally here," I say, attempting to shift everyone's focus to my tardy cousin. Because they're currently all staring at me.

Ro, Dela, and Shay all sport smiles of various types. Shay's is pure amusement. Dela's smile is more of an "awe..." type of warm and friendly smile. Ro's is a total "gotcha" grin, her lips stretched to maximum width while her eyes twinkle with the torment she's undoubtedly planning to dish. Hopefully, she'll wait until we're alone.

"I don't have to ask where your mind was," Ro says,

settling on the chair beside me. "The question is, how far did you and Constantine go last night?"

"*Ro!*"

"Because I drove past him, walking down the street a few blocks down," she continues, "and he looked like one very happy Minotaur. And he always looks happy, but this was next-level."

"Can confirm," Shay says, nodding and raising one hand. "Had a little chat with him in front of the bakery. That man is on cloud nine. Vastly different mood from the last time I talked to him, a few days ago."

"The day he stopped in here to talk to you?" Dela asks, leaning closer. "When things got kind of tense?"

"Mm-hmm." Shay nods, then settles her gaze on me. "Brief moment of tension, that's all. Something was weighing on his mind, and I'm going to take a guess you're the something, and that everything is working out the way fate intended."

"There's that word again," I semi-mutter. "Does everyone in this town believe in fate?"

All three women nod.

"And everyone's okay with having fate determine the course of their lives?" I ask, fiddling with the empty paper cup in front of me. "Because to me, fate sounds like lack of free will or the option to choose. Oh sure, you *can* choose, but going against fate will ruin someone else's life."

The women go silent, all traces of smiling, teasing, or good vibes snuffed out by my opinion.

Dela, sweetheart that she is, reaches across the table and squeezes my hand. "Sounds like your welcome packet included a lot of big stuff."

Ro's snort rips through the tension I unintentionally created. "And now we're back to my earlier question. Just how big was his *stuff*, and how welcoming was your packet?"

Raising both hands as if in surrender, Shay rises from her seat. "I'm out. I cannot be having work conversations with Constantine if I know about his sex life. Though, for the record, I'm happy he's happy, and hope you will be, too." She points her gloved hand at me before giving us all a wave and walking away.

"Is she germaphobic?" I ask, once the coffee shop's door closes behind her. "The no touching, sitting away from us, wearing leather gloves inside during the summer..."

Dela's lips turn down. "Nothing like that. She's a witch. A seer, specifically. When she touches someone, she sees their future and, well, she doesn't want to."

Beside me, even Ro looks serious.

"So, she never touches *anybody?* You know, even personally," I whisper, and they shake their heads. "Wow. That's rough."

"You know who else hadn't touched anyone in a hell of a long time?" One of Ro's ginger eyebrows rises. "Constantine." She nods as if to confirm her own story. "The day he told me you're his mate, he said that once fate has chosen a mate for a Minotaur, they literally cannot be attracted to anyone else, even if they haven't located their fated mate."

Uneasy as the constraints and repercussions of fate make me, my heart picks up speed, knowing I'm that one special person for him. Because there's no denying his attraction to me. Or mine to him. "Did he mention how long he's been waiting for me?" It's a question I should ask him directly, but I'm too curious to wait.

"He said it's been a decade and a half, Nat. That man has gone without for fifteen years."

"Holy shit!" I clap my hand over my mouth, but not before every head in the place turns in my direction.

Across from me, Dela giggles. "For once, it's not me blurting something out and turning red because of it."

"So, last night...?" Ro makes the gimme motion with both hands. "Did you put an end to his long-ass drought? Tell us everything."

Dela makes a lighthearted pouty sound while pushing her chair back from the table. "It's been forever since I've had girl time like this, but I think I have to take a page from Shay's book. I can't be blushing and averting my eyes every time my boss is around."

"Oh, don't go. Please? We'll talk about something else." I give Ro the stink-eye. *Right?*

A bubbly laugh rises from Dela's model-perfect, luscious lips. "That's sweet, but you two need to roll with this convo. Plus, I always call my mom on Saturdays, and I found out she has plans later, so I need to catch her before I miss a day. Believe me when I tell you that you never want to take a single day for granted." Coming around the table, she leans in and gives me a quick hug. "It was so nice to meet you. Text me anytime and no pressure, but I vote for you to stay in town after the wedding."

"Thanks, it was great meeting you, too." I smile until she leaves the coffee shop, then it's just me and Ro, finally. "Your friends seem nice."

"Everyone in town is nice. I'm probably the least nice

person here," Ro says with a snort. "You're way better suited to the vibe than me."

Talk about a perfect segue. "Um, on the subject of vibes, is there a store here that sells them?"

"Heck yeah, there is." She's out of her chair before the last word has left her mouth, hauling me up along with her. "You are going to lose your freaking mind when you see the stuff Lexi sells."

I toss my empty cup in the trash on the way out of *The Brew*, the brilliant morning sun blinding me when we step out onto the sidewalk. I was more than a little distracted with Constantine on our walk over here. Now that I'm taking a good look at the downtown, I see all the things I didn't notice earlier.

The main street is a hub of bustling activity. No empty or rundown stores; everything is pristine and eye-catching. Manicured trees and raised flowerbeds dot the edge of wide, well-maintained sidewalks. Angled parking lines both sides of the street—hatred of parallel parking must be universal. In the center of it all, there's a large parkette with lush green grass, gardens, and benches. A beautiful fountain sits in the middle, and there's a large raised gazebo near one end, its wide stairs facing the length of the park.

I point at it, asking, "That's where the wedding's happening?"

"Yup. But we can talk about the wedding stuff later. Right now, I want to hear the Natalie stuff." Ro hooks her arm with mine, guiding me down the street. "Especially the parts that include you getting your mate bond on. Or *not* getting it on, since you want to buy a new vibrator."

"Why can't it be both? Are you telling me you haven't used a vibrator since moving out here to be with Dak?"

"Damn straight. He insists on being the giver of all orgasms. Literally, *all*." Grinning at me, she wiggles her eyebrows in a hubba-hubba motion. "Even those times when I just want a quick little release O, he takes care of it. The man knows his place, Nat, and that place is between my legs."

Well, I can't say that sounds horrible. And I wouldn't be surprised if Constantine offered for things to be the same way, though I think he'd be less intense about it than Ro's orc fiancé.

Ro halts in front of a small, green-and-purple shop with a gold window decal that reads *Every Witch Way*. "This is it."

"Are you sure? With a name like that, it sounds like an occult shop."

"Oh, there's magic stuff—for getting you magically stuffed," she says, tugging the door open and essentially shoving me inside.

One glance is all it takes for my eyes to feel as if they're going to pop out of my face. There are dildos everywhere. All kinds of sizes, shapes, and colors. "Holy—" I snap my lips closed before embarrassing myself. Again.

"Not so holy, though I do have an angel's cock model that I guarantee you'll find quite heavenly, and some incredibly realistic angel-wing feathers which are fantastic for sensual touch play." The response comes from behind a counter, then the voice's owner pops into view. "Oh! New girl alert! And Rosetta, hi!" The young, green-skinned woman hurries out to greet us up close, thrusting her hand forward. "I'm Lexi, the person to see for all things sexy and wonderfully bewitched."

My gaze drops to her green hand with slim fingers and long, purple nails, waiting for me to take it. "You don't mind shaking hands?"

"Of course not." She grabs hold of my fingers the instant I tentatively raise them. "Why in the realms would I mind shaking hands?"

"She met Shay this morning," Ro says.

"Ah. Well, Shay is a seer, and I'm not, so no visions for this witch." She gives up pumping my hand to gesture at her face, tilting it this way and that, the way a cosmetics model might. "Plus, this is Goodwin green, whereas Shay is a Winterlock. Totally separate covens. Different styles of magic. Mine is more fun." She winks. "What brings you ladies in this morning? Shopping for something magical to spice up the bedroom, or just touring around?"

"Just touring." I jump in before Ro can throw me under the embarrassment bus.

Lexi's ebony hair shimmers with her nod. "Take your time and check everything out. All my products are made from body-safe materials, so if you're wondering about insertion in any or all possible orifices, the answer is, yes, you can." Her laugh seems to bounce in the small shop. "If it fits, of course. Some of the models are rather large, after all!"

My gaze drifts to a massive, heavily ridged, dark-green dildo on a nearby shelf. It must be twelve inches high, and that's not including the big set of balls at its base. It makes Constantine's cock look average in size.

Following my focused stare, Lexi moves to the shelf and

strokes the appendage lovingly. "Forest giant. Isn't he marvelous?" A blissful sigh leaves her lips. "Vern moved from Fate's Falls a few years ago, unfortunately. But his licensing agreement is indefinite, so at least we'll always have his majestic cock in stock."

Wait, what? I can't get any of the questions out because my bottom lip is hanging down.

"Show her what they do, Lexi." Ro gives me a shoulder bump. "This is the coolest."

Lexi gives up caressing the huge dildo to position her palms on either side. "The motions will vary, adapting to the user's physical responses during each use, so this is just for demonstration purposes." The next words she says are in another language. Then the big green dick begins rippling and moving side to side.

"There are no batteries," Ro says. "It's infused with magic."

"But...how? And I mean that in every sense of the word. How?"

A brief utterance later, the dildo stills, and Lexi smiles over at us. "All the models are anatomical replicas created from live volunteers who've entered into a licensing contract. Some people choose a set term, others go infinite, like Vern did. Forest giants live a long time, but by signing an endless agreement, his estate will receive the royalties as long as *Every Witch Way* is in business. It's all legally airtight, and the licensors are paid generously. A mold is made of whatever body part we'll be selling, then the products are individually hand-poured by moi, and imbued with a pleasure-giving spell."

"And you sell enough of them in a town as small as

Fate's Falls to make a living?" The struggling artist in me can't wrap my head around how that's possible.

"Not even close!" Lexi laughs again. "The big money comes from the website. Humans can't get enough monster-inspired sex toys, but you probably know that, right?"

Once again, my cheeks heat. Thank god this particular witch doesn't read minds. Nobody, not even Ro, knows about the tentacle toy I bought last year, after reading a series of super-steamy Kraken romance books. That hunk of silicone went from box to bed to bin in a matter of one day. The definition of disappointment.

"How do you sell to humans outside the protected area without being discovered? And without you there to start them with a spell, how do the products know when to move? And when to stop?"

"The website uses a standard URL humans can access, and the Oracle's magic makes it impossible to track back. The outpost sits just outside the boundary area. It has a variety of valid shipping addresses. They process all the packages going in and out of Fate's Falls. There are lots of businesses here that do very well beyond the border. As for how the magic works... witchcraft doesn't have to be doom and gloom. Human customers believe they're cordlessly rechargeable on the dock provided with each unit, and activated by body heat. It's bullshit, but nobody questions it because the products always work perfectly. Lots of very satisfied customers out there!" she says with a wink. "I'll leave you to explore the goodies."

I wait for Lexi to return to whatever she was doing, ducked down behind the counter, then drag Ro to the farthest corner of the little store. "This is—" When words escape me, I throw my hands up.

"Wild, right? I was so tempted to send you something from here, but I could never decide what kind of monster dick you'd prefer." Again, Ro wiggles her eyebrows at me, then turns her head toward the counter, and calls out, "Lexi, do you have a Minotaur model?"

"Ro!" I hiss under my breath.

"Sure do, ladies!" One green arm shoots up, pointing toward a shelf on the opposite side of the shop. "It's one of the bestsellers!"

Ro drags me in the direction indicated by Lexi's finger. She scans the decorative placards sitting in front of each item, her lips moving as she silently reads the creature descriptions until she gets to the one I'm already staring at. "There it is, Nat. The Minotaur. That's pretty damn big."

"It is."

"There's no name on it—for privacy reasons, I'm sure —but maybe it's Constantine's."

"It's not." *Shit!*

Her head whips in my direction, her eyes popping wide open when she sees what I'm sure is a crimson blush on my face. "You've seen his cock! And had a good enough look to know it's not this one," she says, snorting, dodging when I try to cover her mouth with my hand. "No more with-holding—did you fuck?"

"Can you please keep your voice down?" A pointless ask, I know. Rolling my eyes, I sigh. "None of this—" I make the hand gesture for intercourse. "But yes to other stuff. Good stuff. *Really good.*"

The high-pitched squeal Ro makes has Lexi popping up

behind the counter. "If there's celebrating happening, I want in!"

"Natalie and Constantine are mates!" Ro hugs me tight enough that I'm gasping for air within seconds.

"Not," I sputter, "officially." I take a deep breath when she pulls back, holding me at arm's length. "Don't get your hopes up for me to stay."

"Why *wouldn't* you stay? You hit it off before you'd even met. You've obviously got physical chemistry if you did 'really good stuff' with him the first night, and you never get down with a guy on the first date. Hell, you rarely even get down with a guy."

"Thanks, Ro. Always nice to be reminded I'm uptight."

"Stop that." She gives me a mock slap on the face, complete with sound effects. "I bet it's because you're his mate. Part of you has been waiting for him all this time. And now you found each other. Just...fall in love, make adorable furry babies, and stay here forever. Please..."

"We'd have to have sex to make babies, and I'm not sure it's possible." I tilt my head toward the Minotaur dildo and whisper, "He's bigger than that."

Ro's eyes go round. "Oh my. Well, maybe Lexi has some training dildos you could practice with."

"I do," Lexi says, appearing at our sides, as if out of thin air. "But I don't think you'll need them. Not if fate has mated you to a Minotaur." She reaches for a jarred product on the shelf below the imposing dildo. "Minotaur semen is a known aphrodisiac. It's one of my fastest selling products."

Not much makes Ro pause, but even her mouth is hanging open as she points at the small container between

Lexi's thumb and index finger. "Are you saying that's a jar of Minotaur jizz?"

"With a pinch of magic to maintain its shelf life. No artificial preservatives here!"

"It's a pretty small jar," I say, remembering the amount of cum Constantine produced, and the flow that continued afterward. I probably swallowed three times as much last night.

"Because Minotaur ejaculate is highly potent. Only a small amount is needed to achieve intense sexual results."

Oh shit. "How is it, um…" I try clearing my throat, but there's no getting rid of the sensation there. The memory from last night is so vivid, I can almost taste Constantine's cum in my mouth, feel its silkiness sliding down my throat. "How do people use it?"

"Topically provides wonderful results. It's absorbed into the dermal layers immediately and heightens sensation instantly."

"Damn, Nat," Ro says, grinning widely. "You lucky bitch."

I shoot her the side-eye, then reach for the jar in Lexi's hand.

"You won't need this." Lexi draws her hand back. "Your mate's semen will prepare your vagina for penetration."

This is the wrong place to be getting turned on, but how can I not with images of Constantine smearing his cum onto my pussy running wild in my mind? "Oh, I was just wondering if there were any other directions or warnings on the label."

"The only risk is exhaustion from extreme pleasure!" Lexi laughs while returning it to the shelf, then leans in close enough to whisper in my ear. "Ingestion is completely safe and very exhilarating, but it won't help make his cock fit inside you—you'll need to massage it around down there for that."

"Thanks," I choke out.

"Anytime," she says, winking as she walks away.

I snag Ro by the arm and tug her toward the front of the shop. "Let's continue on the tour."

"What did she say to you back there? And I thought you wanted a vibrator?"

"Not a magically enhanced one that's molded from someone's actual cock," I say, low enough that I hope only Ro hears.

No such luck, if Lexi's laughter as we open the door is any indication.

This town is going to take some getting used to.

Chapter Eleven

CONSTANTINE

It's the best kind of surprise finding Natalie in my backyard when I get home from putting in a few hours' work at the brewery. The urge to head out there directly so I can soak up every possible minute with her is strong. But when I see what she's doing under the cover of a broadleaf maple tree, I pause with my hand on the sliding glass door.

She's drawing. Legs crossed on a canvas lounge chair, back hunched, left hand holding a large tablet in place on her lap, right hand moving quickly across the screen. And her face—gods, her face. Rosy cheeks, pink lips parted, eyes wide open and focused on whatever she's drawing.

She mentioned having to work on commission pieces while she's here. More than once, she also said creativity hasn't been coming easily.

Watching her now, she seems completely engrossed. I should leave her alone to continue, not disturb her groove, but I can't help myself. The next thing I know, the house is behind me and I'm crossing the flagstone patio, my mate in my sights.

Her head rises and turns, an instant, beautiful smile curving her soft mouth. "Hi."

Unable to resist, I dip down for a taste of her lips. An assumption, yes, but she responds by opening for me, not only inviting my tongue into her mouth but also sliding hers into mine. She hums as I thread my fingers through her hair. Softly moans when I cup the back of her head firmly and deepen the kiss. I'm tempted to scoop her into my arms and take her to bed right now, in the middle of the afternoon, and never let her leave.

"Your way of saying hi is much better," she says, when I force myself to break away.

"Think you could get used to it?" I'm pushing, something I keep saying I won't do. I'm beginning to think it's impossible not to push. I want her to be mine, and I know she wants to be.

"I don't want it to stop. Can that be enough for now?" Reaching up, she traces my features, leaving sparks in the wake of her touch, then strokes my hair where it lies in front of my shoulder. "I'm not saying I've decided to leave after the wedding. There's just so much for me to digest before I make a decision that changes both our lives. But I'm really thinking about everything, I want you to know that. When I decide, it won't be impulsive. I'll be sure."

"I couldn't ask for more than that." I curl my fingers around hers and bring them to my lips, pressing my lips to the soft skin on the back of her hand. "I thought you'd be gone most of the day with Rosetta and Dela, checking out the town."

"Dela bailed before we left the coffee shop. Ro's X-rated talk scared her off."

Settling on the end of lounger, I make a show of covering my ears. "Remember—no details about Dakgorim."

Laughing lightly, she leans over her tablet—which powered off sometime during our kiss—and pulls my hands from my head. "Actually, she started talking about you and me. Asking pointed questions. Making guesses based on my face's various shades of pink. Dela and Shay both said they'd rather not know those kinds of details about their boss's personal life."

"Good." The image of them scurrying makes me chuckle. "I'd rather they don't know, too." But I'm damn curious to know how much Natalie shared with her cousin. "What did you and Rosetta do after that?"

"She took me in a few shops, then out to her place to show me her workshop and the baby's room. The workshop is amazing, the best space she's ever had to do her metalworking. And the nursery Dak built is stunning, though I'm still in shock that Ro's pregnant. That she's in love and getting married. I never in a million years thought she'd want those things in her life."

"She found her mate. That changes everything." It needs saying, as many times as it takes. Greeted by silence, it's clear I pushed too much. "Did you get a pretty new notebook at *Fae-vorite Things?*"

Her expression lightens at the subject change. "We didn't get there. I'll go by myself. Maybe tomorrow."

That's a good sign. I want her to feel comfortable here. Like part of the community. But I also won't sacrifice an opportunity to spend time with her. "I'll join you, unless you'd prefer I didn't."

"I'd like it very much if you joined me," she says, sliding her hand across the chair toward mine. "Not just for shopping."

"Whatever and wherever you want, I'm in."

"About being *in*..." The roses in her cheeks are in full bloom now, her irises blown wide, despite the bright afternoon sunlight. "One of the places Ro took me was a shop called *Every Witch Way*."

There's no containing the chuckle that scene inspires. "You met Lexi."

The highlights in Natalie's auburn hair shine with her nod. "She seems like she'd be a fun person to hang out with." No mention of Lexi being a witch, or having green skin. Natalie's initial surprise at the reality of monsters seems to be fully behind her. Behind us.

"Lexi definitely favors fun," I say, stroking Natalie's small, soft hand. "I've always known Lexi to be friendly, easygoing, and good-natured. She's smart, too."

"So, I could trust the information she gave me to be accurate?" That's a loaded question if ever there was one.

"I don't know her on a level where I feel comfortable giving a blanket yes or no answer. But I'd believe anything Lexi says about her products or business. She's very passionate about them, and thorough."

"Then I think you should clear your calendar." Moving

her drawing tablet to a side table, Natalie smiles, then climbs onto my lap. "Because she told me that Minotaur semen is an extremely potent aphrodisiac, and that if you massage enough of it into my pussy, I'll be able to take your cock."

My bullish huff is strong enough to ruffle her hair, which makes her laugh and snuggle closer. "Consider my calendar clear until you beg me to stop making you come."

Her arms wrap behind my neck as I push up from the chair. "Apparently, if I swallow enough of your cum, that might be never."

"You probably shouldn't have told me that, my sweet little mate. Not when you know how much I want to make you mine forever."

She doesn't answer. Not with words. But the way she clings to me, nuzzling my neck and stroking my hair while I carry her into the house... those actions speak volumes. She may not be consciously ready to commit to being my mate, but the desire is there.

"We're going to your room?" she asks when I turn down the hall opposite the guest bedrooms.

Our room. One day, that's how she will describe it. Until then... "Larger bed. More room to spread you out and pleasure you."

"I really can't argue with that." She smiles up at me as I lay her on the bed, my kneeling position spreading her thighs.

The flowy dress she's wearing pools just below her waist, the material thin enough to see her bra beneath, and my mouth waters at the sight of her breasts rapidly rising and falling. I didn't worship them as I should have last night. Time to change that.

"Having trouble?" She gives me a playful, coy look as I struggle to manipulate the tiny pearl buttons running down the front of her sundress.

"There are far too many of these," I say when even the first one proves too challenging for my big hands.

"Then take it off another way, however you need to. I have other dresses."

She doesn't realize the instincts her suggestion provokes —an uncivilized desire to ravage her, to breed her. This isn't the time, but maybe one day, after she has claimed me for her mate, I will let the bullish part of me have his way.

For now, I skim my fingertips along the neckline of the pretty blue dress she won't get to wear again, then curl my hands around the front edges and rip it open in one swift motion. The sound of buttons bouncing across the hard-wood floor seems distant compared to the rumble rolling up from my chest.

"*Natalie.*" I trace the top edge of a pale-blue lace bra, then drag my finger down the middle of her body, to the front of her matching panties. "You're so beautiful. I want to look at you forever."

With one hand, she opens the front clasp of the bra. The material falls away and her breasts spill free. I cup them, one in each hand, learning their weight, stroking the deep-rose nipples with my thumbs until both are tall, hard peaks.

"God, yes," she says when I take the first one into my mouth. "Your tongue feels so good. And your teeth scraping my skin when you suck... and your fur..."

I give the other breast the same treatment, going back and forth between them until her skin is red and slick with my saliva. I would spend hours teasing her breasts, but the scent of her arousal is irresistible. I lick and kiss my way down her body, tugging her panties out of the way when I reach her hips.

She wiggles to help me get rid of them, placing one delicate foot in the middle of my chest as soon as the scrap of material clears her toes. "Now you. I want you naked."

Shirt, pants, and the rest hit the floor in under ten seconds. My cock is hard as a tree trunk, and when she licks her lips while staring at it, every bullish instinct kicks in simultaneously. Rough huffing of breath, stomping of hooves, my tail swishing wildly. Physiological responses I wasn't sure a human mate would be able to get past, but Natalie doesn't just accept them, they arouse her. I see it in her glassy eyes. Her parted lips and shallow breathing. But mostly, in her scent. I could come just from the scent of her pussy.

Cupping her feet, I open her wide, drape her legs over my shoulders, then kneel between her spread legs. "Gods, Natalie. Your pussy is the only thing I want to eat for the rest of my life." I mean to go slow. To tease and draw out her pleasure. But the instant I taste her on my tongue, have my nose pressed tight against her slick, silky folds, there is no slow. No teasing. No control. Just my ravenous hunger for my mate's heat.

Her soft moans and twitching hips spur my need for her to come on my face. I reach down, stroke myself until my fingers are coated in precum, then spread it over her entrance. Her back arches as I burrow my tongue inside her, fucking her with it while I nudge and rock my wide nose against her clit.

I gather more precum, withdraw my tongue and replace it with two well-coated fingers. Her walls squeeze them, resisting, then relax.

"I want some," she says, holding her mouth open while her hips rock against my face, my fingers.

And I want to feed it to her. All day and night long. Feasting on her pussy, I look up at her, press my precum-covered fingers between her parted lips, growling when she moans. My cock is too big to experience the sensation of her sucking it, but I swear I feel it between my legs when she sucks my fingers deeper into her mouth.

I slip my fingers from her pussy, coat them in precum, then slide three inside her while licking and flicking her clit. The air is thick with her scent, her breathy moans. She's ready to come. Desperate for it. But my mate also wants my cock, and I need to ready her. To stretch her for what's next.

I'm already throbbing for her. Leaking a steady stream. I dribble more into her mouth, then cover my hand with it and ease all my fingers between her swollen pink pussy lips.

"Oh god," she pants, as I push deeper. Deeper. Until the base of my fingers sit at her entrance. She moans low and long as I begin to fuck her with my whole hand while doubling-down on her clit. A sharp, high-pitched cry replaces the moan as she tangles her fingers in my hair. Grabs my horns. Bucks against my face, panting and babbling as she rides my mouth, my fingers, my nose.

Even when her grinding stops and her body goes flaccid, I keep devouring her. Twisting my fingers inside her, I find that spot that drove her to orgasm last night, and press on it while rolling my tongue fast and hard over her clit.

Her body arches like a taut bow, then she cries out my name, rocking against my face until her panting turns to soft, breathy laughter. "Tell me I'm ready," she says when I rise between her thighs. "Because I want to be ready."

If I could look at every part of her at once, I would. In this moment, I can't look away from her pussy, stretched and glistening. I guide my cock to her entrance, using the fat tip to spread precum all over her.

She's so small. Even with the stretching, the head of my cock is wider than her opening. But she'll take me. We'll fit. She'll come with my cock buried inside her, and I'll coat her walls with my cum.

She tenses as I press in, rocking forward, forward, trying to push past her body's defenses. Beneath me, her hair moves against the blanket as she shakes her head. "You're too big."

Pulling back may be the most difficult thing I've ever done. For her, I'd do anything. Including not give up.

I lean in and kiss her. Softly at first, then deeper, sliding my shaft over her clit in a matching rhythm, until her legs wrap around my back and her hips rock upward to meet my thrusts.

Her body twitches and tenses, jerking beneath me as she comes again, moaning my name against my lips. "Try again, please, I want you inside me."

"You'll have me there, my sweet one. I promise you." I ease out of her hold. Kneeling before her creamy thighs again, I stroke myself hard and fast, until my balls are hot and tight, my cock throbbing with the need for release. "Taste me."

She reaches down, catching the first small surge of cum, her eyes closing as she licks her fingers clean.

"Again, Natalie." I growl as she happily, greedily, swallows another mouthful. "Watch me fuck you," I command, looking into her lust-drunk eyes when she stares up at me. "Watch us mate." My tail whips as the last trace of control snaps.

She catches it, brings the tip to her breasts, tickling her nipples with the fur. Lips parted, eyes wide, she watches cum spurt from my cock.

I paint her pussy with it, drenching her folds, her entrance, then grip her hips and push inside. No resistance this time; her pussy is ready, pliant. But still so tight. So perfectly godsdamned tight.

Holding anything back is impossible now. My head tips back, a long, loud low leaving my mouth as I sink deeper inside her body.

She cries out, panting, grabbing my hips, her nails digging in. "*Yes, ohh...*"

Buried as deep as her body can take me, I lean forward, rocking, pressing against her clit until her walls squeeze me while she comes. "Gods, Natalie, you feel so good. So fucking good, my mate." Growling, I kiss her as deeply and thoroughly as I'm fucking her, getting lost in the taste of her, the feel of her, the lines between us blurring, meshing.

My mate. Her voice is crystal clear in my mind. The words unmistakable. Her arms wind behind my neck, her fingers thread through my hair, and her gentle sigh fills my mouth.

Breaking the kiss only because I want to look in her eyes, I ease back that small bit, fighting the words that are desperate to leave my mouth. The questions. The declarations. The promise to love her for eternity.

"Did you hear me?" Her cheeks tint with an adorable blush. "In your head, I mean. I'm sure you heard all the other things."

"I heard it all. Your beautiful, sexy sounds and your words through our bond. I loved all of it."

"I did too. And I meant it, meant those words. I know you're my mate, just as much as I'm yours." Emotions swirl in her eyes as she pulls her bottom lip, still puffy from everything we shared, between her teeth.

"But you still haven't decided what the future holds for us."

"I need more time. To sort through things. Not things about us. I know *how* I feel, just not what I'm going to do with those feelings. And until I do..." Her soft fingers trail along my face, my nose, my lips. "It wouldn't be fair for me to commit yet, to claim you as my mate."

Whether she formalizes it or not, verbalizes it or doesn't, I am hers already. I always will be. Telling her that would seem like pressure. So, in this moment, I do what's right for her. I kiss her. And I wait.

Chapter Twelve

CONSTANTINE

The past week went by with the smoothness of silk. Mornings of waking up with Natalie in my arms. Days divided between me showing her around Fate's Falls, or putting in some work while she and Rosetta dive into wedding prep for the upcoming event, or Natalie tapping into what she describes as fresh creative mojo. Hours can go by in a blink when she gets in a drawing groove. And I could sit and just watch. There's something magical about her all the time, but practically glows when she's drawing.

All evenings have been spent together. Some, we grabbed dinner at one of the restaurants in town. Others, I cooked for my mate, pride roaring inside me when she moaned in delight at the food I fed her, especially when she allowed me to hand-feed her.

I love feeding her. Food. My cum. Especially that. I knew it was part of some species' mating practices, but I never had the urge to do it until I met Natalie. Watching the thick, milky substance puddle in her mouth before her lips close, hearing her hum and moan as she swallows... it stirs primal instincts I didn't know I possessed.

Every night together is passion and pleasure, each time easier and deeper than the one before. Preparation no longer required. Her body welcomes mine, eagerly stretching to take me inside. Molding to my cock, milking endless cum from my balls.

Everything is perfect—except waiting for Natalie's decision. With half her planned time here gone, the clock is running down. I swear I hear the hands ticking in my mind, moving faster with each day that passes.

I don't know what I'll do if she leaves. If she let me, I could follow her back to Toronto. Live in seclusion, venturing out under the cover of night, hiding what I am beneath hoods and other coverings. I'd be with her, but I wouldn't be the mate I am now. Would that version of me be enough for her? It shouldn't be. She deserves someone who can take care of her, not an oversized house pet.

"Hey, boss—whoa," Shay says, popping her head inside the back office at *The Brew*, mid-Monday morning. "I was going to tell you Natalie's out front, and that you should pack up whatever work you're doing to go check on her because she looks kind of down, but you look just as bad off. Everything okay on the home front? I have no basis for giving relationship advice, but I'm here if you need a sounding board."

"Appreciate the offer, but it's just something I have to wait out."

Shay nods. "Gotcha." There's a good chance she knows what's going on, without me saying more. Natalie and Rosetta share every detail of their lives, and much of that recent togetherness has taken place in the coffee shop, under Shay's watchful eye and misses-nothing ears.

"Thanks for letting me know Natalie's here."

"Sure thing. I've got your back, you know. Here at work and as a friend."

"Ditto, Shay." I give her a nod, close the programs I was too distracted to actually use, then tuck the chair under the desk and head out front to the customer area.

Every cell in my body wakes up when Natalie enters my view. Her gaze snaps to mine, and she brightens, but not before I see the expression Shay described. Even Natalie's beautiful smile doesn't entirely hide the clouds in her eyes. Doesn't matter that we've only known each other a short time, we've spent it learning about each other. Even without our mate bond, I'd be tuned-in to her emotions. Something's weighing on her. If I can alleviate that weight, I will. Whatever it takes.

"Hi," she says as I pull the nearest chair as close to her as possible and take a seat. Her hands rest on the table, and I cover both with one of mine, completely engulfing them.

I lean in for a brief kiss. Not the kind she prefers, but publicly appropriate. "I thought you were working on a commission piece this morning."

"I was. I started to, anyway. Then I got a call and now I'm here."

"Rosetta wants to do something?"

Soft hair moves like an auburn wave when she shakes her head. "No, it wasn't Ro on the phone. It was my mom."

It's as if a rock dropped into my stomach. I know she's close with both parents, even though they don't live near each other anymore. "Is everything okay?"

"With them, yes. They're healthy and happy, loving their RV life."

"Then why are your beautiful lips curved down instead of up?" I ask, tracing the line of her mouth.

"Apparently, when I told them I was coming out to British Columbia for Ro's wedding, they decided to change course and head in this direction so we could have a visit. A fun surprise because they miss me. Under normal circumstances, I'd be thrilled to get extra time with my parents. They've developed a serious aversion to city settings since they became full-time RVers—" A small, genuine smile tugs at her lips, disappearing just as quickly. "Now, I only see them a few times a year. But they don't know about non-human species and magically protected towns. They won't be able to find Fate's Falls. So, I won't get to see them *and* I'll have to lie to them. I hate both those things. I don't even know what lie I can tell that won't have them calling the police because they think I'm under duress."

"Did you call Rosetta to get her opinion?"

Again, Natalie shakes her head. "Her wedding is this weekend and she just started having morning sickness. I'm not going to add my parent troubles to her plate, especially when hers have dickishly disowned her. Talk about twisting the knife."

"Then we'll solve it together." I cup her face in my hands and look into her eyes. "We'll find a way to make it work."

"I don't know how that's possible. They're near Kalispell, Montana now. They never take the most direct route, but even so, they'll be in Kelowna tomorrow."

Not a lot of time, and honestly, we have limited options. But we do have options. "Come on," I say, standing and drawing her up with me. "Let's go for a walk and talk."

The mid-morning sunshine wraps around us when we exit *The Brew*. Taking her hand, I lead her toward Amazra's bakery up the street. Sugary baked goods won't fix the problem, but a treat might coax a temporary smile to Natalie's face.

"Have you considered telling your parents the truth about Fate's Falls?" It's the question I've wanted to ask every day of the past week. I know fear of estrangement from her parents is the primary reason she's hesitant to commit to our bond. Unfortunate as the current situation is, it has provided the perfect opportunity. "You told me they're both free-spirited, open-minded people. There's a chance they may accept everything that exists, like you did."

"And if they don't, then what?"

"You meet them in a nearby town to have your visit, then return to Fate's Falls for your cousin's wedding."

"And *then* what, Constantine?" Though she's never voiced it specifically, I know it's fear of losing the close relationship with her parents that's holding her back from staying here.

Stopping on the sidewalk, I wrap my arms around her,

nuzzling her hair, kissing her head. Delaying the conversation because I'm afraid where it'll end—with the end.

"We should talk about this." Her soft voice is muffled against my chest, but I feel the hitch in her breath. She sighs as I rub her back, then tips her head back to meet my eyes. "We need to talk about what happens after the wedding."

"Have you made your decision?"

"No," she says quietly.

"Then anything I want to say will sound like I'm pressuring you. And I'm trying very hard not to do that, even though it's killing me not to do everything in my power to convince you to stay."

She buries her face against me, squeezing me as tight as her petite arms around my bulky frame can. Then her muscles relax and her breathing levels out, and I feel her warmth inside me as well as out.

I don't want to lose you.

"You won't," I say, answering the words she spoke through our bond. "We'll find a way. I promise you."

Her eyes hold unshed tears when she eases backward and looks up at me. "You shouldn't promise something that's beyond your control."

"I don't need to be in control of this. Fate is. And I'm sure fate didn't send you to me just to tear you out of my life after I've fallen in love with you."

She blinks slowly, her lips parting and closing, parting and closing. "You're in love with me?"

"Completely."

"Because of the mate bond?"

I shake my head. "Being mated brought us together, but I fell in love with you because you're you."

She jumps into my arms, wrapping herself around me, right there in the middle of town. A pair of vulpine folk make their species' equivalent of a wolf whistle as they walk by, one of them issuing a good-natured "Get a room" loud enough for any monster in the vicinity to hear.

"Sorry," Natalie whispers in my ear, then wiggles her way back to her feet.

"Never apologize for showing me how you feel." I press my lips to her crown, inhaling her scent until it fills every corner of my senses.

"I'll show you in detail at home." Bright pink floods her cheeks. "At your house, I meant. Obviously."

"'At home' works for me." Capturing her hand, I weave our fingers together, using them to point at the store before us. "Let's stop in here first. You never got the pretty pink notebook you wanted."

"To keep track of all the monster information I need to remember," she says as I hold the door open for her. "Do you think me buying one will signal fate to work in our favor?"

I don't get the chance to answer. The moment she crosses the threshold of *Fae-vorite Things*, the fairy who owns the shop makes a beeline—or more accurately, a fairy line—straight for Natalie.

Flora's brilliant-green eyes widen as she hovers in front of Natalie, her iridescent wings moving fast enough to make a faint buzzing sound. She does a circle around Natalie, pausing at her back, then zips in close, lifting Natalie's hair to inspect her ears. "You look fully human."

"Um...because I am?"

"You're part human, for sure, since you have no wings

and your ears appear naturally round." Flora settles in front of us, her wings stilling, but remaining open. "But there's no mistaking that scent. Where in your lineage is your fairy family member? Or members? Can't be too far back. It's strong enough that I smelled it as soon as you stepped inside."

"It must be my shampoo or body lotion you're smelling. I don't have any fairy family members."

"You absolutely do." Flora's wings whir, lifting her off the floor again. "Come with me," she says over her shoulder, "we'll look them up in the registry."

Instead of following, Natalie leans in to me and whispers, "Is this a joke she plays with new people?"

"Only if it's a new joke."

"She didn't do this with Dela or Ro?"

"Definitely not with Dela. You'll have to ask Rosetta next time you talk to her."

"Let's go do that now." Natalie turns toward the door, only struggling a little when I wrap my arm around her waist and prevent her from escaping. An adorable *hmph* pushes through her lips. "I'm getting a weird vibe in here, and the only non-human I want to vibe with is you."

I manage to contain the audible part of my amusement, but not the smile on my face. "We'll go straight home after this, and I'll give you all the vibrations you can handle."

"Fine," she says, grudgingly taking a step toward the rear of the shop, where Flora is waiting with a big smile. "Let's get this crazy over with."

Flora claps as we reach the counter. "This is so exciting. We haven't had new fairy blood in Fate's Falls in over four decades. I'm Flora, by the way." She shoves one delicate-looking hand out. "Ooh!" Her pointed ears twitch when Natalie accepts the handshake. "Did you feel that little spark?"

"The static electricity shock?"

Fairy laughter has a certain lightness to it, and Flora's practically floats. "No, sweetie, that was fairy magic!"

Natalie backs up tight to my body, tilting her head to give me a *help me* look. I wrap my arms around her, covering her hand with mine and squeezing gently.

"What's your full given name?" Flora asks, fingers poised over a computer terminal keyboard.

"Natalie Aine Somers. Natalie is the basic spelling, nothing funky. Last name is spelled s-o-m-e-r-s and the middle name is a-i-n-e."

"What a lovely Irish spelling. Is that from your human side of the family, I wonder, or the fairy side?"

There is no fairy side.

I bite back a chuckle at the words Natalie pushed to my mind. Even in my head, her frustration is clear.

"Of course there is," Flora says, looking up from the computer. "I've got the information right here."

Natalie goes stiff as a board in my arms. "Wait—you heard me? You—*heard me?*"

"Well, you did broadcast it, sweetie. Toward your mate, yes, but when in the company of fairies, anything you push his way might as well be through a loudspeaker. Something to keep in mind, so you can keep your private things private." She winks.

The tension goes out of Natalie's body. As in, all the tension, all at once.

"Uh-oh, I think I short-circuited her." Flora rises higher

above the counter to get a closer look at Natalie's rag-doll slumped position in my arms. "Take her into my apartment at the back, Constantine. I'll get her a cold drink."

I scoop Natalie into my arms, holding her tight as I follow Flora through a door and down a short hall that opens into the living room of Flora's small apartment. By the time I settle on the couch with Natalie on my lap, she's blinking and looking around. "I'm here," I say, "you're safe."

"Is it true? Am I part fairy?"

"You fainted before we got details, but it sounds like it." I stroke her hair, everything in me warming when she leans in to the touch. "It would explain how naturally we're able to share thoughts with our bond."

"I do like that part." Her soft lips curve in a smile. "I like all the parts."

"As do I."

"Okay, here we go," Flora calls before fluttering into the room. Giving us a little heads-up, no doubt. She hands Natalie a highball glass of clear, bubbly liquid. "Plain old sparkling water. Not even a pinch of fairy magic."

A strangled sound leaves Natalie's lips, then she croaks out, "Thank you." With each sip, Natalie perks up a bit more, her normal rosy tones fully restored by the time she reaches the bottom of the drink.

"Feel better?" Sitting sideways on the opposite end of the couch, Flora's wings move in slow, gentle rhythm. "Ready to explore your fairy roots?"

"My fairy roots." Natalie shakes her head. "Of all the things I've learned since I got here, I think this is the most unbelievable."

"Well, believe it. Fairies are fastidious record-keepers. We write everything down."

My chuckle gets both women's attention. My smile is for my mate. "You said that to me the first time we talked. 'I write everything down.' Maybe it's the fairy genes."

Across from us, Flora beams. "Could be! Natalie, your great-grandfather on your father's side, Alfred Somers, is a full fairy. He was born and raised in Wildefell, Montana, a magically protected mountain town like this one."

"Montana?" Natalie jerks upright, staring at me wide-eyed. "Is it coincidence my parents just spent a week there?"

"Your great-grandfather still lives in Wildefell," Flora says. "Maybe they were visiting him."

"I have a living great-grandfather? And he's a full fairy?" She's not technically screeching, but with each question, the pitch of her voice gets higher. "Wait—do male fairies have wings too?"

"Of course," Flora says, fluttering her wings fast enough to lift her off the couch. "Even being only half fairy, your grandfather had wings. But then he mated with a human woman, further diluting the fairy genes, and by the time your father was born, there wasn't enough fairy DNA to produce wings. It's noted in the records."

"Holy shit." Natalie flops back against my chest. "Just... holy shit."

"What about Rosetta?" I ask. "Is she part fairy too?"

Natalie shakes her head. "No, we're related on my mom's side. Oh my god, do you think my mom knows about my dad's fairy heritage?"

I can't send a telepathic message to anyone but my mate, but the look I give Flora above Natalie's head seems to do the trick, because Flora doesn't speak, though I'm sure she knows the answer to Natalie's question. "I think there's one way to find out," I say, rising from the couch and guiding Natalie to her feet. "Let's go home and call your parents."

Chapter Thirteen

NATALIE

"Did you know your grandfather? The half-fairy one?" Constantine asks as we step inside his house. He's been peppering me with questions all the way here.

I think he's trying to make sure I don't pass out again. Apparently, shock and I don't mesh well. "I only ever talked to him on the phone. He and my grandmother lived far away. My parents said they couldn't travel, and I always assumed it was for health reasons. Now I know it was because my grandfather had wings. Wings!" I recognize the hint of hysteria in my laugh. I had it the day I met Constantine. After everything that's happened, you'd think I'd be handling this better. "They told me he died, but I wonder if he's still alive, too." Okay, not the best train of thought for remaining calm.

"From everything you've told me about your parents and your relationship with them, if there was any dishonesty on their part, I'm sure it would've been to protect the family, not to deceive you."

"I know." I lean in to his side, my arms circling his waist as much as possible while we walk through the house. "This is just so much to absorb. My family includes *fairies*. It's…"

"Amazing. Exciting." In the living room, he wraps me in an embrace, his big hand stroking my hair while turning my ear to his chest. The steady thump of his heart calls for mine to slow and match it. "And good news for us, I hope."

It could be, if the conversation with my parents goes the right way. But even if my mom is aware of my dad's unique lineage, she may not know about all the other non-human species in existence. Aside from wings and pointy ears, fairies basically look human. My Minotaur mate, on the other hand…

Making the call, broaching this subject matter, is a risk. One I don't have to take. I could lie to my parents, tell them Ro and her fiancé eloped, that there's no wedding to attend. I could meet them in Kelowna for a visit, come back here for the wedding, then go back to Toronto without breathing a word of this reality to my parents. I could reject Constantine officially, freeing us both to move on, separately.

Even if I leave here, I won't forget him. I could never replace him. I don't want to.

I know what I *do* want.

Tipping my face up, I meet his waiting gaze. His strong jaw is clenched, his black lips in a straight line. I don't have to ask if he heard my thoughts. He wouldn't have, since my mind is the furthest thing from open to him right now. I've been locked up tight in my own head since we left Flora's. No more of that. I want to share everything with him. Always.

Placing my palms on his big, broad chest, I inhale deeply and open myself to him. Light flickers in his amber eyes, then warmth flows through me, igniting sparks of arousal and calm comfort at the same time. Our bond. Our connection. Reaching deeper, I picture the door between us. Open it.

I decided. I'm staying with you.

His eyes widen. "Gods, Natalie. Tell me I heard you correctly." The smile that breaks across his face when I nod is like no other I've seen.

"I wanted to tell you before I call my parents, so you know I choose us, that my staying isn't because they approve. I'm staying because I want to, whether it's easy or not. I hope this call with my parents goes smoothly, but I know we'll sort things somehow. I'm not going to lose them because I love you. Tell me what I need to do to make it official. How do I accept you as my mate—no, how do I *claim* you as my mate? Because I want to. I love you."

That open door in my mind feels like it blows off the hinges, leaving a wide-open archway in its place. Where there was light before, there's a beautiful, perfect, endless glow.

"You just did," he says, then dips down, sealing his lips to mine.

The call can wait.

His chuckle rumbles against me.

I don't have to ask if he heard my thought. I know he did. Everything is clear now. Right and perfect.

Claim me as your mate.

Mine. His single unspoken word takes all the space in my mind, sending my pulse rocketing, the heat between us flaring. The pressure of his kiss intensifies, his growl vibrating through me as his tongue slides between my parted lips.

Our hands bump and tangle as we scramble to get rid of the physical things between us. Clothing hits the floor, some intact, some shredded by Constantine's big, impatient hands. Clothes are replaceable. Time with him isn't.

After a week of seeing him naked, you'd think I'd be used to the sight. Wrong. I can't take my eyes off him. He's huge. All over. Wide and thick, solid from horned head to hooves. Dark-brown fur covers nearly every inch of him, and I run my hands over it, spreading my fingers. The soft fur tickles the tender skin in the V between each finger, and I swear a feel it between my legs too. Longing tugs beneath my clit and deep inside me. I need his huge cock filling me. Making me come. I'll never get enough of him.

His tail lashes wildly behind him, his hoofs stomping against the hardwood as I grip his cock with both hands and stroke it hard. An actual blowjob is impossible, but I drop to my knees and do the next best thing, licking up and down his long, impossibly thick shaft, sucking each of his big, heavy balls between my lips and tugging until he groans.

One hand threads through my hair to cradle the back of my head. With the other, he grips his meaty cock and angles it toward my mouth. "Open for me, my sweet little mate. Taste me."

Starved for him, always, I open wide, humming when the first drops of sweet, milky cum hit my tongue. He presses the bulbous head of his cock against my lips and presses, forcing my lips to stretch wider. Wider. As open as my mouth can go, leaving no gap for air. Breathing through my nose fills my head and lungs with his rich, earthy, masculine scent. I wait until thick warmth coats my tongue, all the way to the back of my throat. Then I close my lips before anything seeps out, moaning as I swallow it all down. The light, buzzy sensation hits me faster than the times before. Because we're truly mated. Because I love him.

Looking up at him, I stroke him again, gathering precum on both hands, then spread it over my nipples and between my legs, where I rub my clit until my hips are rocking against my fingers. I'm drunk on him. Desperate and so, *so* ready.

His nostrils flare, his breath pushing out in a rough huff. My sexy Minotaur doesn't attempt to hide his bullish side from me now. He knows it turns me on. Everything about him does.

He reaches for me, helping me to my feet, then lifts me onto the couch, placing me on my knees, facing away. The firm pressure of his palm on my heated skin as he bends me over the backrest sends anticipation rippling through me.

I'm expecting him to fuck me, but he doesn't. He pushes my knees apart—wide apart—then settles between them, face up. His thick, furry arms wrap around my thighs and he pulls me down onto his face. My eyes roll back in my head as his long, wide tongue pushes inside me, so incredibly deep. Another bullish huff pushes from his nose, the heat of it tickling my sensitized skin.

I moan as his tongue finds that magic spot and moves against it, pushing me toward the peak. Reaching down, I take hold of his horns, gripping them hard while I rock against his face, rubbing my clit hard and fast on his wide nose.

Wet warmth slides down the crack of my ass, then the pad of his finger is there, massaging my anus with his precum. Getting it ready to take his thick finger.

Leaning forward, angling so I'm open wider, I moan as he presses the tip past the tight ring. "More," I pant, "I want all of it." I moan as his finger fills my ass—deeper, deeper, then I cry out, riding his face hard while I come and come and come.

"Gods, you undo me, Natalie," he says, rubbing his precum-covered cock head up and down my pussy after positioning himself behind me. Holding my hips, he pushes inside, huffing, his hooves clomping. Driving me wild with all the primal tells of his desire for me.

Knowing he'll fit doesn't make the absolute stretch of it any less thrilling. My panted moans join his rough grunts of pleasure. Every inch feels like it must be the last, but there's more. So much more. It should be too much, but I want it all. Inhuman sounds leave me when he bottoms out, his furry abdomen pressed tight to my ass cheeks and heavy balls brushing my inner thighs.

He folds over me, his chest to my back. Slips his hand between my legs to stroke my clit. "You take me so well. I crave you. More than air, I need you." His normally smooth voice is husky with tightly held need. "Come for me, my sweet mate. Squeeze me, milk every drop from me."

Stars explode behind my closed eyelids as I come hard, panting his name, writhing against his fingers on my clit, my skin tingling beneath his hot, ragged breath on my neck.

His deep, long low fills my ear as he comes. His massive cock throbs inside me, then I'm coming again, my body flying high on cum coating the deepest parts of me.

His cock slips out of me, and what feels like endless cum oozes from me, running down the insides of my thighs and—

"Oh no, the couch," I say, shifting quickly, but it's too late. Puddles of white are all over the earthy-gray velour. "Yikes. That's going to leave a mark."

Constantine's rumbling silent laughter vibrates through me as he pulls me against him, then onto the other side of the L-shaped couch, where he lays us out together in a beautifully entwined embrace, nuzzling my hair and neck before kissing me softly. "All that matters is the mark you left on my heart, sweet Natalie."

"It matches the one you made on mine," I whisper, snuggling in, soaking in the rightness of being with my mate.

The call, and everything else in the world, can wait a while longer.

The next day

NATALIE

"They're still not picking up," I say to Constantine after my third attempt to call my parents. "Twice yesterday, and now this. I keep getting their voicemail."

"But they replied to your text last night. They're probably going through spotty service areas."

Nodding, I set my phone down. Logically, I know he's right. My parents have never been the kind of people to be glued to their phones. Tech is a convenience, a means to be in touch with me, not part of their daily lives. Especially since they downsized their possessions and stress levels and hit the road. More than ever, they're all about slowing down, taking the path less followed, and connecting with the world around them. They'd probably love it here in Fate's Falls.

I may have inherited some fairy DNA from my dad, but I did not get the "relax and be chill" gene from either parent, so I pick up my phone and check it again. No missed calls. No new voicemails. I tap the group text I have with both of them, rereading our exchange from last night. Well, *their* exchange, really. They're honestly the cutest.

> Hi, Mom! Hi, Dad! I can't wait to hug you! And I have news. Great news. Call me when you get to Kelowna so we can arrange a place to meet.

Mom:
Hi honey! We're planning to do some night driving so we can get to you sooner. Love you!

Dad:
Don't worry, I'm doing the night driving, not your mom. The wildlife population is counting on me.

Mom:
It was one raccoon, fifteen years ago. And it ran out in front of my car as if it had a death wish. My poor little Toyota was never the same.

Dad:
I'm still doing the night driving.

Dad:
See you tomorrow, sweetie! Can't wait to hear your news!

Constantine is right. My parents are fine. They're not avoiding my calls, just driving along and watching the world go by. They'll phone when they get to Kelowna, then I'll head down and meet them. I'll tell Dad I know about his fairy heritage, then share my great news—I have a fated mate! I'm in love with a Minotaur! No big deal. Except it's a huge deal. A tall, furry, horned and hooved, huge deal.

I slump over the kitchen island, my forehead pressed to the cool granite. Constantine's hand on my back settles my anxious mind instantly, each gentle pass up and down my spine further easing the tension.

"Are you expecting Rosetta?" he asks when the doorbell chimes.

I sit up straight, checking my phone again to see if I missed a message from her. "No. We're not getting together until tomorrow afternoon to make wedding favors."

His heavy brow lowers over narrowed eyes. "I don't know what 'wedding favors' are. That must be a human thing."

"Or just a chick thing. Flora and Shay knew."

A smile takes the place of his perplexed expression. "I'm happy you're building new friendships."

"Me too. I already have more friends here than I did in my entire lifetime when I lived in Toronto." I scrunch my nose when he smiles wider. "What?"

"I like hearing you describe it as 'when I lived in Toronto.' Putting it in the past tense. No longer calling it 'back home.'"

I hop off the counter stool and wrap my arms around him. "This is my home now."

"I'm glad you feel comfortable in Fate's Falls."

"I do, I really love this town, but I was talking about you. Wherever you are, that's my home."

"And you are mine." He dips down, brushing his lips over mine. The beginning of a kiss that could quickly become more—if the doorbell didn't chime again.

Groaning, I ease backward from his arms. "Sorry, that has to be Ro. With everything happening in her life right now, I don't want to leave her hanging, even though she didn't let me know she's coming."

"I'd never want you to." He presses a kiss to my forehead. "I'm glad she has you, and she's always welcome here. Just don't give her a key."

"Um, never." My body heats at the thought of all the things I wouldn't want anyone to walk in on. So many perfectly dirty things. "I better get the door," I say, when his nostrils flare and his tail swishes side to side. I don't need to hear his thoughts to know he can smell my arousal, that he'd like nothing more than to make me come right now.

"*Natalie.*" A bullish huff of breath follows my name. "The door or our bed. Five seconds."

Giggling, I take one more look at his big, beefy deliciousness, then hurry to the door. I don't even try to tone down the love-drunk smile on my face as I grab the handle. Ro will take one look at me, give me a "get it, girl," then turn around and leave us to our insatiable mate bond. I'll make it up to her. I have all the time in the world with her now.

Only...it's not Ro's face I see when I open the door.

"Surprise!" my parents say in unison, complete with jazz hands.

I shriek at the sight of them—and not in a good way. My distress call brings Constantine thundering to the door, the sound of his hooves clapping against the hardwood practically echoing.

He pulls up just shy of barreling into me, his big arms wrapping around me protectively. Warmth flows through me from a place deeper than his physical embrace. Our bond. *Everything will be okay.*

What should I do?

"Introducing us would be good," Dad says, giving me a big smile while openings his arms. "Hi, sweetie. We sure have missed you."

Happy tears roll down my cheeks as I go from the arms of my mate to those of my father. Two men I love and trust. Both here in this strange, wonderful place where unbelievable things make perfect sense.

"Dad," I say, hugging him tight. Then, "Did you *hear* my question?"

"I did. Only to break the ice, since you seemed pretty flustered. I'll do my best to block your internal voice, but do your old dad a favor and try not to share any overly personal thoughts with your boyfriend while I'm around."

Choking on a laugh, I ease out of the hug. "Okay, but he's not my boyfriend. Constantine is my mate. My fated mate."

Mom's eyes open wide, then she takes her turn at attempting to hug me to death. "That's wonderful, sweetheart. Your dad and I are so happy for you."

"You are?" I ask as we break apart.

"Of course we are," Dad says. "Finding your other half is the best kind of magic." He wraps his arms around Mom, gazing at her as if he's seeing her for the first time. "I knew your mom was my fated mate immediately."

"We both knew," Mom says, touching his face and drawing him in for a kiss.

Watching them share a kiss isn't awkward at all. They've never hidden their affection for each other. Knowing what I know now about the mate bond, it's a miracle I never had to witness more than G-rated shows of love.

"Love you," Dad says to her, then turns to me again. "Now that you've found your special one, your mom and I will always know you're happy, safe, and loved, whether we're on the opposite side of the continent or parked in your driveway."

I glance past them to the RV—the first one I've seen in Fate's Falls, with good reason. "How did you find me? How did you find Fate's Falls?"

"You told us where you are. Fate's Falls may not be on human maps, but it's on fairy ones, which are much better kept, for the record."

"Of course they are," I say, feeling lighter and luckier than ever in my life. "We fairies write everything down."

"That we do, sweetie." Dad extends a hand to Constantine, a warm grin in place as they shake. "Jonas Somers. And this is my wife, Siobhan. We're honored to meet you."

"The honor is mine entirely," Constantine says, nodding at each of them. "Thank you for creating your beautiful daughter. I will treasure, respect, and protect her for the rest of my life."

Who needs a wedding when your mate makes a vow like that on the front doorstep? Though...Constantine would look hot in a tux, and I can't even imagine what honeymoon sex would be like.

Marry me and find out.

Biting my lip doesn't hide the big smile overtaking my face. Nothing could. My life is officially the best fairytale ever.

Epilogue

Eight Months Later

CONSTANTINE

If Dakgorim had his way, Rosetta and their new baby would be off-limits to everyone but him. His protective nature went into overdrive when Rosetta got pregnant, ratcheting even higher when their orcling arrived. Delivery by home birth, and if not for having a female physician available, Dak might've insisted on playing doctor in addition to head of security.

That was a week ago. It's taken Rosetta seven days to convince Dak to let us visit.

Natalie has been climbing the walls at being kept away.

No amount of cute pictures would satisfy her—and by gods, there've been a lot of them.

But we're here now, bearing more gifts than any single baby needs. Dakgorim will undoubtedly scowl at the sight of so many bags and boxes. Orcs are minimalists by nature. Pretty sure Rosetta wouldn't give a damn if we brought a truckload or came empty-handed. She just wants to see Natalie.

My mate is practically vibrating beside me by the time I knock on the door of the small wooden home in the forest. Her smile falters a bit when Dak opens the door. They don't dislike each other, but he's not the easiest person to get close to, whereas Natalie is warm and open to everyone. Including Dak. Even now, while he's scowling and sniffing the air around us, giving us the orc equivalent of a black-light check over.

"You may enter," he says, stepping aside.

"Congratulations!" Smiling—genuinely, too—Natalie offers him a light-blue envelope, which he takes after an awkward moment of silent glaring.

"You may leave the packages out here." He points toward an empty corner. "No clutter in the nursery."

"Okay, sure," Natalie says, as the two of us set our armfuls of gifts in the designated space. "Is Ro going through another feng shui phase?"

Dak's thick black eyebrows draw together, then he jerks his head toward the addition he built last summer. "Follow me."

Natalie catches my hand, squeezing it while opening herself to me. *She must love him for his huge dick.*

My body shakes with silent amusement at the thought

she sends me. I know she doesn't really believe her cousin is with Dak for his cock. In the eight months she's been in Fate's Falls, she's witnessed the bond between Dakgorim and Rosetta many times. She's seen how naturally they click, despite their many obvious differences in personality. Fate chose well for both of them. And now they share more than their mate bond. The urge to have that with Natalie has been there since our first night together. Maybe one day, when she's ready.

Dakgorim enters the nursery ahead of us, moving to stand behind Rosetta where she's lifting the swaddled baby from the crib Dak made. The orc's facial expression softens as he looks at his wife and child. He even smiles, as much as an orc can.

A soft gasp leaves Natalie's lips as she moves toward them, tilting her head to get a better look at the sleeping green orcling in her cousin's arms. "Oh, Ro, he's so beautiful."

"Want to hold him?" Ro asks.

"Of course, I do." Instead of taking the babe from Ro's arms, she looks up at Dak. "I will be as careful with him as I would with my own child." Not asking permission, per se, but an offer of respect. She really has gotten to know the big orc.

"I know you will," he says, nodding.

Happy tears roll down my mate's face as Ro places the infant in Natalie's arms, arranging his blanket just so. "Oh, Ro... he's utterly perfect. And he smells so good."

"Come back when his diaper's full." Ro snorts. Then sighs, stroking the red hair that lies across his small forehead. "I'm kidding. Even his toxic-level poop doesn't bother me. I love him so much, Nat. I can't even describe it."

I move closer, pressed to Natalie's back, one hand on her hip, the other on her shoulder. I offer congratulations to Dak and Rosetta, keep my focus on the baby in Natalie's arms, but ignoring her scent is impossible. Arousal. Love. And...ripeness?

I stopped taking the pill. And I'm ovulating.

It takes conscious effort to control my Minotaur physiology. To hold my tail and hooves still. To prevent my breath from huffing out.

My mate feels it all, though. Her soft laugh rings in my mind, as clear as if she released it in the room.

Take me home and put a baby bull in me.

My cock feels hard enough to break down the walls. My heart, so full it could burst. But this could be an impulsive decision made in a moment of baby lust. As much as I want to see her grow round with our baby, I don't want her to have regrets. *Are you certain you're ready?*

Tipping her face up to look at me, she smiles. *I'm ready for everything with you.*

And that's what I will always give you, my mate. Everything.

Thank you for reading Natalie and Constantine's
fated-mates romance! I hope you enjoyed your visit
to the magical monster town of Fate's Falls!

Go back to Fate's Falls now and
read Dela and Razbunare's fated-mates romance in
The Grumpy Demon's Sunshine.

Shay gets her happily ever after in ***A Reaper is Forever***.

Join my mailing list and stay up to date on new releases,
bonus content, sales, freebies, contests, and more.
www.karladoyle.com/newsletter

Read more of Karla Doyle's monster romances:

Now You See Me (Screaming Woods)
Snake Believe (Screaming Woods)

A Troll in the Hay (Harmony Glen)
Rock 'n' Troll (Harmony Glen)
Wood You Be Vine? (Harmony Glen)

Mated to the Minotaur (Fate's Falls)
The Grumpy Demon's Sunshine (Fate's Falls)
A Reaper is Forever (Fate's Falls)
The Rhino's Rose (Fate's Falls)
A Dash of Demon (Fate's Falls)
Hell's Belle (Fate's Falls)
Orc-ily Ever After (Fate's Falls)
Falling for the Yeti (Fate's Falls)
and more to come...

Once Upon A Beast (Hemlock Woods)
The Beast Within (Hemlock Woods)

Leaping Into Love (Monsters of Rita's Hollow)

FATE'S FALLS

STEAMY AND SWEET MONSTER ROMANCES

Go on an adventure to the secret town of Fate's Falls and fall in love with all of its irresistible monster mates! All books take place in Fate's Falls, and you'll see some character appearances and familiar town landmarks. Each book is a standalone romance with a different couple and their journey to a very happily ever after.

The Grumpy Demon's Sunshine
Mated to the Minotaur
A Reaper is Forever
The Rhino's Rose
A Dash of Demon
Hell's Belle
Orc-ily Ever After
Falling for the Yeti
To Merry a Grumpy Minotaur

...and more to come!

Contemporary Romances:

Wedded Miss

Dad Bod Wingman (Hope Harbor)

Heart Beats (Hope Harbor)

Last Call Casanova (Hope Harbor)

Fleshing It Out (Hope Harbor)

The Deal With Love (Hope Harbor)

Doggy Style (Hope Harbor)

Resorting to Love (linked to Hope Harbor)

White Lie Christmas (linked to Hope Harbor)

King of Her Dreams (Hope Harbor)

Heart of Texas (linked to Hope Harbor)

Her Pipe Dream (Hope Harbor)

12 Days (Hope Harbor)

Puck That

Shifting Gears (Under the Hood)

Driver's Seat (Under the Hood)

Gingerbread Man (Man of the Month: Candy Cane Key)

Just in Queso (Man of the Month: Magnolia Point)

Unexpected Addition

Dating the Doubter

Gift Wrapped

Cup of Sugar (Close to Home #1)

Icing on the Cake (Close to Home #2)

Sweet as Candy (Close to Home #3)

Body of Work (Very Personal Training #1)

Worth the Wait (Very Personal Training #2)

Game Plan

More Than Words

Crossing the Line

Visit Karla's website for the most up-to-date list:

www.karladoyle.com

See Karla's books sorted by themes and tropes:

www.karladoyle.com/books/by-tropes

About the Author

A small-town girl with some big-city experience, Karla resides in Southwestern Ontario with her husband. She studied fashion design in college and spent 20+ years working in that industry before succumbing to the writing muse. When she's not writing the sexy stories that  swirl around in her head, you can find her spending time with family, hanging out with book-loving friends on Facebook, or cuddled up with a book and her adorable pets.

Karla loves hearing from readers! Connect with her online, or send her an email: karla@karladoyle.com

Join Karla's mailing list to stay up to date on all her news: www.karladoyle.com/newsletter/

facebook.com/KarlaDoyleAuthor

instagram.com/KarlaDoyleAuthor

tiktok.com/@karladoyleauthor

bookbub.com/authors/karla-doyle

goodreads.com/karlad

youtube.com/@KarlaDoyleAuthor

patreon.com/karladoyleauthor

bsky.app/profile/karladoyleauthor.bsky.social

amazon.com/author/karladoyle.bsky.social

This book was written by a human.
Every sentence came directly from the mind of the author.

**This author does not use
or support AI-generated content.**

www.ingramcontent.com/pod-product-compliance
Lightning Source LLC
Chambersburg PA
CBHW060415310726
48976CB00003B/1054